Me and My Hittas 2

Tranay Adams

Me and My Hittas 2

Me And My Hittas 2/ Tranay Adams-1st ed. © 2016

ISBN: 978-1-7377789-6-7

Email: dopereadzpresents@gmail.com

Facebook: Tranay Adams

Instagram: Tranay Adams

Cover Artist: Divine

Chapter One

Nightmare had rallied his troops and so had Pavielle. With drive-bys and walk-ups being executed on both opposing sides, bodies were dropping like flies and piling so high you could build a wall out of them. Pavielle was feeling the loss of every homie he lost but there was the death of one homie that really hit home for him.

Big Panic made his way out of Wally's Liquor Store with a brown paper bag in his hand. Its contents were a bottle of Alize, a box of Swishers, a box of Magnums and two clear plastic cups. The big man was overly excited; he had some ass on the line he had been trying to get for a month now; a little fine, educated honey by the name of Remy. He had been trying to get baby over to the house, but she seemed to always have an excuse. If she wasn't at school, she was at work, or taking care of her grandmother or babysitting her niece and nephew.

Panic was about to say fuck it and move along to this other broad he had bumped a week ago until he got a call from her out of the blue. He worked his charm and got her to agree to get a motel room with him. With images of her voluptuous, curvy body burned into his mental, he thought about how he was going to wax that ass like Mr. Miyagi. The thought alone had his dick nudging at the zipper of his jeans, trying to free its self.

Panic was so caught up in the XXX movie playing within the theater of his mind that he hadn't spotted the two suspicious characters that had followed him in and out of the store. They had clung to the shadows and masked up with their chrome Uzis. When the big man went to stick his key into the key-hole of the driver side door, he saw their reflection in the window. His eyelids peeled wide open and his mouth formed an O as he gasped. The killers had their automatic weapons out stretched and were about to spray him. He whipped around quickly, dropping his bag of goods while in motion; he reached for the strap on his waistband. But it was far too late; the masked assassins already had the drop on him. Their Uzis fired in unison, waking up the silent night as bullets struck their mark, misting the air with his blood. Panic danced on his sneakers as the bullets entered him and exited out of his back, splattering his blood against the side of his ride. It looked as if the bullets were attempting to levitate his three-hundred pound body from the surface. Panic crashed to the asphalt in the liquor store parking lot, landing hard on the ground. His blood ran from under him and mixed in with the alcohol that was concealed inside of the Alize bottle. The masked gunmen fled into the night, letting the darkness swallow them whole.

Urrrrrrrrrrk!

The tires of a Turquoise '95 Honda Civic squealed as it bent the corner of the liquor store in a hurry, making a clean getaway. The killers pulled off their ski-masks and revealed their identities: the driver was Supacrip and the nigga in the front passenger seat was Nike. Supacrip kept a constant look over his shoulder as he sped ahead, one gloved hand gripping the steering wheel. While he was occupied with this, his partner-in-crime was hiding the murder weapons inside of a stash spot.

"You see The Ones, Cuz?"Nike inquired.

"Nah, we good." Supacrip assured him.

"Smooth."

With that said, Supacrip slowed the G-ride to a modest speed that was sure not to break any speeding laws. Once he felt that they were in the clear, they breathed easily. Having accomplished the mission, they disposed of the Uzis and burned the getaway car.

Kill, kill, kill, murder, murder, murder!

Later that night

Pavielle lay in bed asleep beside Vayda. His cell phone's screen lit up and it danced across the nightstand as a call came through. The young kingpin stirred from his sleep and turned on the lamp light. He checked the caller I.D, pressed talk and brought the phone to his ear.

"What's up, Blood?" he asked groggily into the cell phone, wiping his eyes.

"Panic's dead." He spoke with a dead serious voice.

"Woo, it's too late at night to be playing, fam."

"I'm not playing, Bleed. Real spit, they hit'em tonight."

"Who?" Pavielle looked alive. His elevated voice stirred Vayda from her sleep. She narrowed her eyelids as she looked at him. By the look on his face she could tell something was terribly wrong.

"Nike and Supacrab," Woo told him, his voice slightly cracking under his emotions. "On Lil' Face it's on now, Blood, me and Big Head 'bout to murder every last one of these niggaz. Dinosaurs ain't gon' be the only mothafuckaz that's extinct, on the set."

"Y'all chill for a sec," Pavielle began, sitting up in bed, "I'm a sic old girl on lil' homie. I'ma call her in the A.M and get the ball rolling, alright?"

"Alright, Blood. I love you, my nigga."

"I love you, too, Duce Owe. Twenty minutes." he disconnected the call.

"Boo, what happened?" Vayda asked concerned, scratching her chest as she peered through narrowed eyelids.

Pavielle shut his eyelids and put his hands together in prayer, having a moment of silence for Big Panic. When he peeled his eyelids open, his eyes were glassy and attempting to accumulate tears. Seeing the hurt in her man's eyes, Vayda sat up in bed and took him by the face staring into his eyes. "Babe, tell me what's wrong, what happened?" she inquired, looking as worried as ever.

"My best friend was murdered tonight." He told her, and as soon as he spoke the tears jetted down his cheeks. He shut his eyelids for a moment and bit down on his bottom lip, nostrils flaring.

"Panic?"

"Yeah, go back to sleep, baby." He kissed her on the forehead and then cupped her face, kissing her on the lips. He then turned off the lamp and rolled over to go back to sleep, his heart heavy with grief.

The crown was proving to be heavier than Pavielle thought. Sure he was making more money than he'd ever dreamed of, but it came at the cost of his peace of mind as well as his loved ones. He started to think that his new status was more trouble than it was worth. He truly was paying the cost to be the boss.

Two hours later

Pavielle stirred awake and looked to Vayda, who was sound asleep. He brought his hands down his face and took a deep breath. Big Panic's death was weighing heavily on his mind. He knew that he wasn't going to get any sleep that night so he decided to step outside for a breath of fresh air and a blunt. After throwing on a hoodie and Dickie shorts, he proceeded out of his bedroom.

Pavielle stepped out onto the front porch and closed the door behind him. He took the blunt he'd rolled from behind his ear and stuck it between his lips, sparking it up. He tilted his head back and released a cloud of smoke into the night's cool air. That's when he heard 'Psssst' for his attention from the right side of him. In a flash he whipped that thang off of his hip and swung around, pointing it in the direction that the voice came. At the end of his barrel he found a neighborhood crackhead by the name of Rudy. She was in a burgundy hoodie and dirty, tattered jeans that were torn at the knees. As soon as she saw the Death Dealer in that nigga'z hand, she threw her hands up into the air.

"Whoa, be easy, Booby, it's me." She said, voice shaky with terror.

"Who the fuck is me?" his face tightened with anger and he gripped his banger tighter.

Quickly, she pulled the hood from off her head and revealed her head of half braided hair. It was nappy and unkempt like it hadn't been done in quite some time.

"Rudy."

At the mention of her name, Pavielle tucked the steel back inside of his waistband and went about his business of smoking.

"What's bracking, Rudy?" he threw his head back and blew out a gust of smoke.

She cleared her throat with a fist to her mouth before continuing, "I heard about Panic tonight, I gotta say I'm sorry for your loss." He nodded his head, but didn't look in her direction. His eyes were glassy and he was afraid his hurt would come sliding down his face. "You know the streets are talking and they're saying that it was Nightmare that ordered that hit."

"Yeahhhh, I know." He took the blunt from his lips and tapped it, dumping ashes. The grayish black flakes and embers floated to the ground.

"I know where you can find him."

When she said this, Pavielle's head snapped in her direction and he stepped off the front porch. He closed the distance between them, seriousness spread across his face.

"Where?" he watched as she fished around inside of her jeans pocket. She pulled out a slip of paper and handed it to him. It was an address. He looked it over and then looked back up at her. "What's this address to?"

"His house."

"Alright, what chu won't for this?"

"Nothing," He frowned and narrowed his eyes. "Look, a lotta these mothafuckaz around here treat me like a smoker, but Panic treated me like I was somebody…a human being…a person." Her eyes misted because his death affect her greatly. The big man would bless her with crack, clothes and money for food from time to time. Hell, he'd even paid off a debt to another hustler that she owed so that nigga wouldn't kill her. Thinking about all of this, she wiped the tear that threatened to trickle off the rim of her eye.

"I Griff you," Pavielle nodded.

"Just promise me one thing."

"What's that?"

"You put one right through that nigga'z head when you find him." She gritted, teardrops falling. He gave her his word and pounded his fist to his chest. "Thanks. I gotta go." She sniffled and wiped her eyes with the dirty sleeve of her hoodie. She then threw the hood over her head and walked off down the street where she was joined by another crackhead. Pavielle watched the pair as he smoked his blunt, blowing smoke clouds. Once he was done, he dropped the roach to the ground and mashed it out under his corduroy house shoe. He retreated back inside of the house with one thing on his mind, vengeance.

***

Killa Dre scaled the fence of Inglewood cemetery high and drunk out of his mind. Jumping down to the other side, he staggered forward and fell to all fours. Slowly, he got to his feet searching his person. He was relieved that he hadn't dropped the 40 oz of Olde English malt liquor, but when he searched his ear for his half smoked blunt and discovered he'd lost it, he was disappointed.

"Shit!" he cursed.

Wide eyed, his eyes scanned the grounds for the blunt he'd dropped. When he didn't see it, he shut his eyelids and took a deep breath. "Fuck it." He ran his hand down his face and pulled his bottle of cheap alcohol from where he had it stashed. After twisting off the cap, he took it to the head, guzzling it. The bubbles floated to the bottom of the bottle as his throat rolled up and down his neck. Taking the 40 from his lips, he wiped his mouth with the back of his fist. Shortly thereafter, he shuffled forward drunkenly. Using the illumination from his cell phone, he searched the cemetery's grounds until he found his deceased brother's grave stone. Coming across it, he put his cellular away and stepped to it.

"'Sup with it, big bro?" He took the 40 oz to the head, guzzling it and pouring some out on the lawn below his brother's marble stone. Having screwed the cap back on his alcoholic beverage, he went on to talk to his late sibling. Once he wrapped up their conversation, he made him a promise that he was definitely going to keep.

"The next time you see me here, big bruh, I'll have your killer's blood on these hands," he held up his hands and looked between them. After balling them into fists, he focused his attention back on the stone with his brother's name carved in it. "I swear to God…," his vision was quickly obscured by the tears that accumulated in his eyes, outlining the rims of them. The teardrops fell, hitting the grass and the tip of his right sneaker. "No," he sniffled and snorted back some of the tears that wanted to fall. "No, I swear to you, I'ma kill that nigga."

Killa Dre's older brother, Tramel, was murdered in cold blood outside of his high school after winning a game he and his team played against a rivaling school. The incident tore The Johnson family apart and left the young nigga searching the streets for his sibling's killer. Although he hadn't caught up with him yet, when he did he was going to make him regret the day that he was born.

Thunder rumbled and lightening flashed, hiding his face in darkness and then revealing it, each time it made an appearance. Suddenly, rain fell from the sky looking like falling crystals. Killa Dre threw on the hood of his jacket and sat the Olde English bottle down beside his big brother's marble head. Stashing his hands in his pockets, he turned around and trekked back from where he came.

***

Killa Dre's mother lay across the couch. She was under blankets and fast asleep. Her eyes were swollen from crying and her nose was red. Lying against her chest was a portrait with its back visible. Her hand dangled off the side of the couch just above a box of Kleenex, which sat among an abundance of soiled, balled up tissues. The TV's blue illumination flickered on her face like a light show.

Killa Dre stood where he was observing his mother. He had to admit that she was the strongest person he had ever met. After the loss of his older brother and his father he thought that she'd definitely end up in a straight jacket inside of someone's asylum, but to his surprise, and hers as well, she'd managed to keep it together. Taking a deep breath, Killa Dre staggered forward like a Walking Dead extra. He was still as drunk as a sailor, but he had enough wit to do what he had in mind. He took the portrait from his mother's hand and looked at it. A smile stretched across his lips when he saw that it was a picture of their family. He took the time to admire it for a time before sitting it on the shelf. Afterwards, he placed his mother's hand back upon the couch, covered her up with the blankets, and then turning off the television. He made his way inside of his bedroom where he kicked off his sneakers and pulled off his hoodie. Slinging it aside, he killed the lights and plopped down on the bed. Once he steepled his hands behind his head, he stared up at the ceiling and took a deep breath. An amused express crossed his face as he thought about the look on his brother's murderer's face once he finally caught up with him and filled that ass with lead.

The next morning

"Thank you." Black Jesus said to his maid, Marisol, as she sat his breakfast and his cup of coffee down on the table before him. He slipped on his glasses and opened up the news paper, reading over it. The doorbell chimed, but he didn't bother to tell Marisol to answer it. The paper held all of his attention. Besides that, he already knew she'd get it, because it was just one of the tasks that he was paying her to do. Although he was focused on his reading, that didn't stop him from over hearing the locks being undone on the front door and the maid greeting Tango as he crossed the threshold.

"Jesus Christ, are you, okay?" he overheard her. This caused the drug lord to frown. He folded his paper in half and set it aside.

"I'm fine," he heard Tango say as he made his way through the living room. "Where's the jefe?"

"In the kitchen."

Black Jesus turned around just in time to see his body-guard making his way toward him. He looked like he'd been through hell and back and his arm was in a sling. When he saw this, he immediately thought, Oh, shit. The old gangster didn't even have to say it, because right then he already knew that his shipment had been hit.

Black Jesus' face balled up and he removed his glasses, sitting them aside on the table. He glared at Tango and said, "I wanna know who hit my shipment, and I wanna know now. So you for damn sure better have a name for me."

Tango nodded and said, "I do…Booby."

"Booby?" Black Jesus' brows furrowed, he couldn't believe what his ears were hearing. This couldn't be true, or was it?

"Yes. I'm afraid so." He hung his head like he was sorry to be the bearer of bad news, his hand brushing back and forth up his injured arm. His eyes looked up at his boss to see that he was wearing a devastated expression across his face. This expression quickly morphed into one of anger.

"Alright, I wanna know exactly what happened. And don't chu leave out a single fucking detail." His face balled up as he wagged his finger at him.

"Okay."

Tango went on to recount the story of how Black Jesus' shipment had been jacked. Once he was done God's son seemed to be extremely pissed. His jaws were pulsating as he clenched his fists, veins bulging at his temples.

"Alright, you can leave now." He picked his news paper back up and continued his reading.

"Well, what do you plan on doing about this?"

"Don't worry; I'll take care of it."

"You don't want me to send a hit squad after him."

"I said that I'll take care of it…you're dismissed, Tango. Leave now, your presence sickens me." If it was one thing Black Jesus hated it was failure no matter what the reason was behind it. He never took it too well.

"Boss, I'm sorry. We did our best to protect the shipment but we were overwhelmed." He tried to plead his case. "Those niggers were coming from everywhere."

The kingpin adjusted the news paper as he continued his reading of it. "Tango, if I have to repeat myself again, you and I are going to have ourselves a situation."

Tango took a deep breath causing his shoulders to rise and fall. His eyes lingered on his boss before making his way out of the kitchen, headed for the front door. He didn't know what Black Jesus had in store for Booby, but he was sure as hell glad that he wasn't him.

May the Lord have mercy on that poor bastard's soul, Tango thought to himself as he closed the door shut behind him.

Chapter Two

The next night

"Aye, them squares you hit me off with is fire. Niggaz have been blowing my cell up for the shit." Taco informed Nightmare, rubbing his hands together greedily. The gangsta crip smiled. He was happy to hear that his new product had the streets buzzing. "Only thing is I've had to slang the shit to my Westside ninjas and the few homies that are still fucking with us. The smokers won't come within a hundred yard radius of our traps since we've been beefing with the Twinkies, they're scared they're gonna catch a hot one and shit."

"How much of the shit you got left?" Nightmare asked, taking a peek inside the shopping bag of cash his little homie had given him when he came inside of the house.

"Two. After that I'm sitting on that bullshit Omid gave us. I can't give that shit away. The smokers aren't fucking with it. I can probably pawn the shit off on these outta town niggaz I've been fucking with. I'm not tryna hit our people off with this shit, we're just now getting our mojo back." Nightmare nodded his agreement, massaging his chin. "But on another note, what's up with chu, Cuz? You're getting bigger than a mothafucka," He threw playful punches at his big homie. "Gotta gut, growing an afro and shit. Fuck is going on, nigga?"

"I've been lying up in the house for the last few weeks eating and shit, man." He rubbed on his potbelly. "I'm tryna stay outta these streets, so a nigga won't get caught up."

Nightmare had been laying low since the beef kicked off with Booby. He had started it and he was for damn sure going to finish it. See, the gangsta crip had been losing a hell of alot money since the young kingpin came into the drug game. Pavielle had a better product at a cheaper price that brought all of the fiends from Nightmare's hood sniffing around his way. This had Nightmare hot. He came to the realization that the only way for him to put him and his squad back on top was to slaughter the opposition. With his mind made up, he ordered attacks on Pavielle and his organization. His crew took some hits and so did the other side. As of now the odds of winning seemed to be even, but Nightmare was looking to tip those scales in his favor.

"I feel you." Taco said with a dead serious look.

"Peep this," Nightmare tapped him to get his attention and pulled a slip of paper. He showed him the address and smiled wickedly.

Taco's forehead creased with lines and he said, "What's this?"

"The address to Booby's crib, Cuz. That smoker bitch, Ruby, gave it to for a couple of grams." He stashed the slip of paper back inside of pocket. "You know what time it is now, right?"

"Hell yeah."

They gave one another a pound.

Pavielle was a dead man walking.

Later that night

The lights inside of Starz made the scenery a crimson red. Two Brazilian vixens worked the stage as a tag team. One wore her hair flat-ironed while the other wore hers in a peacock hairstyle. They both had light brown eyes and honey complexions. The pair was stacked and as thick as a couple of stallions. They had matching Double D bust lines and 45 inch asses. They were twins. The only way you could distinguish them was from the mole just above peacock's lip.

The exotic duo was putting on quite a performance for their audience of thirsty, trick ass niggaz. Things had gotten so hot and steamy while on stage that some pervert in the front row whipped out his dick and started jerking off. The strip club's hulking bouncers had to be called to throw the horny mothafucka out.

Tango's four man crew was making it rain $100 dollar bills, smoking Kush and popping bottles of Ace of Spade. Each man had gotten serviced by a dime-piece of his choosing throughout the night. The team was living it up and having the time of their lives.

The night winded down and Tango found himself playing the bar. He took pulls of his cigar as he watched his crew out on the floor, smoke wafting around him. He had been offered everything from a lap dance to a blowjob that night but he had passedup on it all. He wanted some time to reflect on the biggest lick his crew pulled off the day before.

Flashback

The sun was shining its brightest even with it being partially cloudy, its rays were still able to bless the streets with its warmth. The road was quiet save for the Mac truck speeding ahead and leaving debris in its wake. Its driver was a middle aged, portly Mexican man with his baseball cap pulled low over his eyebrows. He listened to a Spanish radio station, twisting a toothpick at the corner of his mouth and drumming his stubby fingers on the steering wheel, in tune with the beat thumping through the speakers. Occasionally, he'd glance at the old Timex watch that adorned his wrist, trying to keep up with the time. The way it was looking he would be right on schedule to make the delivery he was hired for.

Armando Socorro was making more money working for Black Jesus than he ever did with his regular gig. If it wasn't for the fact that he was using his job as a cover up then he would have given up his legal hustle altogether. Making two runs didn't too much bother him though. Two incomes were always better than one. A person could never have enough money, that's for damn sure.

Armando's eyes took a tour of the road, continuing to drum his fingers and looking about, nodding his head to the music. A smile spread across his face thinking about how he was making easy money. For thirteen years now he had been making runs for the South American drug lord without a hitch. He kept an automatic shotgun on deck in case some asshole got it in his head to try to rob him of the precious cargo he was transporting, but thanked God he didn't have to use it in all of his years of service.

Armando's head snapped to the rear view mirror where he saw a speeding Honda Civic coming up. His forehead deepened with lines and he wondered where the hell whoever behind the wheel of that car was going in such a hurry. Thinking nothing of it, he shrugged and went back to viewing the road, this time singing along with the music playing from the radio. An eerie feeling came over him and he looked to the side view mirror once again. The Honda was closer and driving unusually fast. Armando leaned closer to the reflection and felt it in his gut that something was about to jump off. With that in mind, he took the shotgun from the passenger seat and laid it in his lap. Next, he popped open the glove box and removed the box of shells. He opened the lid and sat it down on the seat beside him. His weapon was already cocked and loaded for the drama. Turning down the music, he took his shotgun by its pistol grip handle.

The Honda pulled up alongside him and its front passenger, a brown skinned man wearing a black bandana over the lower half of his face, stuck a MP-5 out of the window at him.

"Pull over, pull this motha..." the passenger was cut short when Armando responded with his shotgun. Bloom! "Ahh, fuck!" he ducked down as the pellets marred the passenger door, tattering the side view mirror. The Honda slowed down trailing a couple feet back but not before receiving another blast from the trucker's powerful weapon. The second blast took the hood of the opposing vehicle off, sending it flying backwards.

"He took a shot at chu?" Tango asked from behind the wheel. He was wearing a bandana over the lower half of his face, too.

"Hell yeah, that prick took a fucking shot at me. Cock sucka," he scowled, gripping both handles of his weapon.

"Slide up on him again, I'ma heat his mothafucka cabbage up, on God."

Armando grabbed his pistol grip shotgun. Pressing the slide of the weapon against the steering wheel, he quickly cocked it with the hand that was commanding the truck. Popping shit in Spanish, he stuck the powerful weapon out of the window, blasting like it was legal. Hearing a bump at his right, his eyes shot to their corners and he went to whip around. His eyes bulged and his next breath caught in his throat when he met a man wearing a black bandana over the lower half of his face, leaving his menacing eyes on display. He was hanging outside of the front passenger side window with a sawed off shotgun pointed dead at his ass, ready to knock the candy out of his piñata (his brain out of his skull).

"Como estas," he greeted him with a wicked smile. "Toss that piece outta da window...slowly." Armando did as he was told, glancing back and forth between the nigga with that thang on him. "Good, now keep yo' eyes on the road." Seeing that his demand had been met, he climbed inside of the truck through the window, being sure to keep his tool on his ass. "Pull this mothafucka over to the side of the road, papi."

"Okay, okay," a petrified Armando nodded his head rapidly, his hands trembling on the steering wheel. His forehead creased with lines when he saw the Honda Civic pull up ahead

of him and saw the other cat that had his gun pointed at him, sitting on the window sill. The man smiled triumphantly holding a finger to the ear bud in his ear.

"Yo, Man Man, you good?" Nate inquired.

"Easy does it, homeboi." Man Man held his finger to his ear bud. Looking ahead he saw the car that he'd used to scale the side of the truck that Barry and Julio were in. It was a Honda Civic, too. It was identical to the one Tango and Nate was aboard. Only it wore a dull black paint job.

"Smooth," he replied. "Take it home."

"I gotchu faded."

Armando pulled the Mac truck over to the side of the road and raised his hands up, they shook uncontrollably. He shut his eyes and swallowed the lump of nervousness that had accumulated in his throat, beads of sweat forming on his forehead.

"P...please, don't kill me...I have a wife and..." Bloom! The roar from the sawed off splattered half of Armando's melon and smacked it up against the window. His brain and chunks of flesh slid down the window and rested at the sill. Man Man, leaned over and opened his door, kicking his dead victim out into the road. He then jumped down to the asphalt just as Nate and Tango were approaching him, guns held at their sides. They opened the shutter of the Mac truck, allowing

Man Man to climb inside. He opened a box to find a large vase inside. He cracked that bitch open with the butt of his sawed off. It crumbled and revealed six kilos of cocaine inside with a black Jesus Christ on it.

Present

A smile broadened Tango's face as smoke billowed out of his nostrils. His squad had managed to pull of the heist and it was looking like they were going to be able to get away with it, too. He was sure that Black Jesus had bought his story. And the gunshot wound that he claimed he received from trying to fight off the bandits from lifting the load helped his case. He was glad he had Nate wound his arm and shoot up the car because it made the web of lies he spun believable.

Black Jesus was responsible for a great amount of the cocaine that entered the United States. During his thirteen year reign the drug lord had made well over five hundred million dollars. This was a wealth that Tango desired to obtain through any means necessary. He concocted a scheme to wipe out his boss and his organization, so that he and his team could take over. Once this was done he would helm the throne and rule his empire with an iron fist.

His first call of action was to assemble his crew so that they could hit Black Jesus' shipment of coke before it could reach its destination. He had it in mind to do this because he knew that without any weight to supply the streets with there would be a drought; a drought that he aimed to capitalize off of. He could set out bricks for whatever price that he wanted and make a killing.

Not only that, but this would lead Black Jesus to believe that he had a formidable enemy; one that he had to eradicate as soon as possible. With no one there to take the blame for what had happened, Tango had to give the drug lord someone that he could believe would try him. That's where Pavielle came in. While Black Jesus and Pavielle's crews were busy warring, he would use this window of opportunity to murder out what was left of both squads before claiming what he felt was his.

The ball of this plan was already in motion. He already bartered a deal with this Chinese plug that would allow him to flood the state with so much coke you could go skiing on it. Now all he had to do was sit back, relax, and wait for the first shot to be fire that would kick off the beef between Black Jesus and Pavielle.

Drink in hand, Money Making Nate staggered to the bar and sat on the stool beside Tango. Nate was a handsome cat with an athletic physique. He rocked a close fade and a thinly trimmed mustache. He had a charm and a smile that could convince a lesbian to open her legs to him.

"What's up, boss man?" Nate flashed his million dollar smile, dimpling his cheeks. "All this ass flocking around and you ain't tryna get none?"

"Nah, I see the bigger picture, so I'm plotting." Tango took the cigar from his mouth and released a roar of smoke.

Nate stared at Tango with a look of confusion. "Man, I know you're not thinking about sticking this mothafucka up with all the paper we're making."

Tango got up from his stool laughing and shaking his head at how ignorant his god son was. "I'm plotting to take over the world," he made a 360 degree turn with his good arm open. "Are you with me?" he asked Nate with his good arm still open, looking for an embrace.

"'Til the end," the handsome young man embraced Tango. He then whispered into his ear and said, "Let's take this mothafucka for all it's worth."

"That's what I like to hear," Tango gripped his shoulder. "I love you, Nathan."

"I love you too, godfather."

"Good boy." He patted him on the cheek like a mafia wise guy. They then sat back down on their respective stools.

"Yo, man, I've been meaning to thank you for hooking up my boy with them thangs." Nate cracked a grin.

"No problem," He waved him off like it wasn't a big deal. "It was a favor. We're family. Family looks out for one another. Am I right?"

"Yeah," Nate nodded in agreement as he raised his glass, "to family."

"To family," Tango clinked his glass into his god son's and took a sip of his alcoholic beverage. "Listen, you assembled the guys we need to pull this thing off?"

"Yeah, I got'em; bunch a buck wild ass Mexican mu'fuckaz. They're cut throat too, use to work for some cartel over there in Tequila Land, but when the head honcho got his head busted they fled over here to avoid persecution from the opposition. Niggaz down though. They're ready whenever we are."

"How many are there and what's their quota?"

"It's six of them lil' mu'fuckaz, man, they're about yay high," Nate held his hand about four feet above the floor. "They want three-hundred kay for the job and guaranteed positions within this thing of ours." He motioned his finger between himself and his godfather.

Tango nodded his head and relit his cigar, blowing more smoke. "Before I give the nod on this, I wanna thorough background check on these guys. You hear me?" Nate nodded yes. "For now, I'll keep to Jesus' program; we wouldn't want him getting wise to our little plan before we've hatched it."

A nice little number that was blondee and thick in all of the right places approached Nate. She was in a skimpy, skintight white leather getup with "6 inch clear heels. She sat on Nate's lap and moved her ass up and down his crotch, causing his dick to bulge. "Ooooh, is all of that for me?" she giggled and smiled, then whispered something into his ear.

"Oh, I'm sorry, sweetheart, but I can't. I'm shooting the shit with my godfather right now, maybe later."

"Aw," White leather said with sad eyes and pouty lips. "You promise?"

"I promise." Nate grinned.

"Don't keep me waiting too long." White leather wrapped her hands around her potential trick's neck and kissed him on the cheek. She then hopped up off his lap and went on about her business.

The handsome young man shook his head as the stripper walked away, disappearing into the atmosphere of the club. "Man, is there anything in this world money can't buy?" he asked Tango, looking away from the white broad that was trying to get him to break bread for what was between her legs.

"Three things," Tango held up three fingers, "Loyalty, love, and respect."

"Fuck y'all doing over here, shawdy?" Man Man asked in a southern drawl as he approached the bar holding a golden bottle by the neck. He was a little tipsy. The slim, brown skinned dude was an Atlanta, Georgia native, Nate's cousin, and a member of Tango's crew.

"Shit. Chilling; chopping it up." Nate answered as he bopped his head to the infectious sounds of Juvenile's *I got that fire*. "Where's Barry and Julio?"

"Barry is out there on the floor for that pussy eating contest and that nigga Julio is somewhere in the back getting his sex pistol polished." He burped.

"Damn, nigga!" Nate frowned and fanned the fumes of cousin's repugnant breath.

"My bad, Cuz, a nigga on tilt out this bitch," He took the bottle of Ace of Spade to the head. Tango looked at Man Man and shook his head. "What? What I do, Tango?"

"Nothing," Tango answered, "absolutely nothing."

Just then Barry approached the bar with the lower half of his face glistening, holding up the crisp $100 dollar bill he had won in the pussy eating contest. "Bottoms up! The drinks are on me!" he told his crew. They all doubled over laughing, holding their stomachs.

Chapter Three

Boom!

Woo kicked the front door of Nightmare's home open with brute force. It flung open and a chunk of the door's frame went flying across the living room. He came in first, holding his banger at his side with both hands. He was wearing a hoodie over his head and a red bandana over the lower half of his face and so was Big Head, Killa Dre and Gouch, who'd came in behind him. Woo gave the signal for them to fan out and they made their departure throughout the house, searching high and low for the gangsta crip. Clear, clear, clear, they sounded off from the respective rooms of the house that they were inside. The entire time there was a dog barking viciously from inside of the kitchen. The homies reassembled at the living room. Woo pulled his bandana down from the lower half of his face and poked his head in the front door's doorway. He gave a sharp whistle and motioned for someone to come inside. A moment later, Pavielle came strolling in dressed in a Raiders beanie and wearing a neoprene mask on the lower half of his face. At his side, his gloved hand held tight to a .9mm that he was hoping to put Nightmare's murder on. He looked to Woo and he took a deep breath, shaking his head no. Pavielle shut his eyes and massaged the bridge of his nose, bowing his head. He shook his head, frustrated that he couldn't track his greatest enemy down. Suddenly, his face twisted with hatred and he swung the butt of his weapon into the lamp that sat on a small table in the corner of the room. It broke apart and the shade went flying off to the side.

"Fuuuuck!" he threw his head back and hollered out his frustration. At that moment, he became quiet having heard the dog barking from inside of the kitchen. He sped walked toward the kitchen and when he crossed the threshold, he found Karma barking and snapping at him. She was chained to a pipe underneath the sink. He could tell from hostile behavior that she'd tear him apart if she could get a hold of him.

Big Head, Killa Dre and Gouch stood in the doorway watching their fearless leader as he stared at the pit bull that was snapping and growling at him. A thought ripped through Pavielle's mind and a sinister smile broadened across his face. *I remember this punk ass dog. That nigga loves this dog.*

Pavielle pointed his .9mm at Karma as she continued barking at him, ignorant to the danger that she was in. Abruptly, he blasted on the hound. It yelped after the first shot, but the next five it didn't even feel. Lowering his smoking banger, Pavielle stared down at the corpse he'd just created amusingly. Without taking his eyes off of his kill, he called out to Big Head who stepped forth.

"Hit this mothafucka up, let him know that we were here." he commanded before turning around and walking out of the kitchen. Woo and Gouch looked on as Big Head tucked his burner on his waistband and pulled a can of spray paint from his back pocket. He got right to work, doing what he loved with his tongue hanging out the side of his mouth. He'd always lost himself inside of his work when he got started. Once the little big head nigga was done, he stepped back and looked up at what he'd done proudly. His homies looked on at what he'd created. Satisfied, Big Head stashed the can of spray paint into his back pocket and threw his hoodie back over his head before casually walking out of the kitchen, his squad bringing up the rear.

Spray painted in bold, bleeding red letters on the wall inside of the kitchen was *The Infamous Eastside Outlaws Rollin' Twenties Bloods.*

***

When Nightmare pulled up in front of his house and saw that the front door had been kicked open, he immediately grabbed his Desert Eagle from beneath his seat and threw his whip in park. Together, he and Taco hopped out and stormed the front yard. They entered the house with watchful eyes and guns ready to blow a mothafucka away. The first thing he noticed was the broken lamp over in the corner but everything else seemed intact. That's when it dawned on him that he didn't hear Karma barking. Immediately, he fled towards the kitchen calling out his pit bull's name. As soon as he met with the dead body of his dog at the center of the kitchen floor, his heart dropped down into the pit of his stomach. Instantly, tears flooded his eyes and his bottom lip shook. He dropped his gun and got down on knees, crawling over to karma, teardrops hitting the linoleum along the way. He ignored the blood as he smeared his knees and hands in the pool that she was lying in. Sitting down, he whimpered like a little boy who had found his goldfish dead, pulling the lifeless animal into his arms. He kissed it on its head and stroked the side of its face lovingly, rocking back and forth. He tilted his head all of the way back, making wrinkles beneath his chin visible as he stared up at the ceiling, tears rolling out of the corners of his eyes, dripping to the surface.

When Taco stepped into the doorway of the kitchen all he could do was shake his head shamefully. Niggaz was fucked up for killing his homeboy's dog, but he understood their get down. Everybody was fair game in war, except families, but he had a feeling after finding Karma dead, that Nightmare was about to break that rule and he'd want him right there along-side him.

"Whyyyyyy? Oh, God, why? Not Karma, not my bitch!" he sniffled and whimpered, snot threatening to drip from his nostrils. "They're dead, baby, they're dead, all of them bitch ass, slob ass niggaz. That's on the set." he whispered into the dog's ear before kissing it on the mouth twice. He then hugged it to his body and shut his eyes, rocking back and forth. He did this for a time before getting to his feet and draping a blanket over it. He scooped the dog up and turned to Taco, dry white tears staining his cheeks, eyes moist and pink. "Follow me into the backyard, Cuz, I'ma bury her and then I'ma make sure that nigga Booby buries something he loves." Taco nodded and followed his big homie out into the backyard where they grabbed a couple of shovels out of the shed. Together, they dug up a six foot plot and buried Karma. They both bowed their heads as Nightmare said a prayer for her. Afterwards, the gangsta crip got cleaned up and they hit the streets to make Pavielle feel his pain.

Nightmare turned down the block of the address that Rudy had given him, keeping an eye out for the house he was looking for. He went down several homes, but the one at the end of the street was the location listed on the slip of paper. It was a two story white house with a charcoal gray rooftop. He smiled evilly when he came upon it, nodding when Taco asked him was this the spot. Parking in the alley, they donned ski-masks and tucked their bangers. Scaling the gate, they hunched over and moved in to carry out their mission. Whoever was inside was going to be a casualty of him and Booby's war, serving as a message to him.

***

A violent kick at the back door startled G-momma. Gasping, she whipped around with big eyes and a slackened jaw. The door rattled twice more before the fourth kick sent it flying open and splinters flying across the room. Nightmare came speed walking through the backdoor, his dangerous eyes peering through the holes of his ski-mask. He was clenching his teeth and gripping his chrome Desert Eagle. G-momma was frozen in shock. She tried to move but her legs wouldn't cooperate with the thoughts her mind commanded. She went to scream but Nightmare swung that thang up against her dome. The impact of the weapon opened up a nasty gash on her temple. It oozed burgundy blackish blood and she went slamming down hard against the linoleum. She lay there wincing and struggling to push her way up from the surface. Her attacker circled her slowly like a leopard taunting its prey, his vengeful eyes staring down at her.

"Old ass bitch," Nightmare harped up phlegm and spit on the elderly lady and kicked her hard as shit in the side, feeling no remorse for her. As far as he was concerned her hands were just as dirty as her grandson's and for that she would pay dearly, very dearly.

"Don't move. I'll be right back." Nightmare marched up front and opened the door for Taco. He shut the door quietly behind him and took the rope from him, waving him along as he headed back inside of the kitchen. He told his little homie to grab G-Momma's wrists while he grabbed her ankles. Together, they placed her on top of the kitchen table. Taco stood aside watching him tie the old woman's wrists and ankles to the legs of the kitchen table. G-Momma's eyes were rolled to their whites and she moved her head from left to right saying God knew what because neither of them could under-stand her. The young hustler observed with a furrowed brow as the gangsta crip ripped open the old lady's gown, revealing her ample bosoms. He tore that off and then her panties, exposing her nappy graying bush.

"Fuck are you about to do?" Taco looked at him to her ex-posed sex then back again, hoping he didn't have in mind what he thought that he did.

"Fuck you think, Cuz." He placed his banger on the table beside his intended victim and unzipped his Dickies, pulling out his penis. Next, he spat in the palm of his hand and began stroking his meat to its full potential.

"Aww, hell naw, Cuz, I know you not about to do what I think you're about to do?" His brows furrowed further and he bit down on his bottom lip hard, placing one hand on his hip while he held his heat down at his side.

"I'm doing exactly what you think I'ma 'bout to do, lil' nigga." He opened up her hairy, flabby legs and climbed on top of the table, looking down at her wearing a sinister smile. G-momma's face was turned to the side and her eyes were still to their whites, she was constantly groaning in pain. Nightmare placed soft kisses on her neck and cheek as he hovered over her continuously stoking his dick, making sure it was good and hard. He stared down into her face as he held himself. Smiling devilishly, he jammed himself inside of her violently, causing her eyelids to shoot open and her mouth to unleash a devastating scream that felt like needles piercing him and his little homie's eardrums. Quickly, he smacked his hand over her mouth and bored into her moistening and accusing eyes, raping her vagina unmercifully.

"Uh! Uh! Uh! Uh!" he went up and down her rapidly, head bobbing and forehead sweating. "Old ass bitch, you gon' take dis big ass dick, unh huh! Love it! Love it! Uh! Uh! Uh!" His smiling face reflected in her pupils as she looked into his face, tears pouring down her cheeks. She tried to scream louder and louder but his dry, calloused hand muffled any sound that attempted to escape. Her lower lips began tearing and seeping blood, lubricating his dick and allowing him to slide in and out of her easily. "There we go, momma, now ya loosening up, get use to the dick, it's good for you. I bet grand daddy wasn't laying it down like this, was he? Was he, bitch?" he scowled and fucked her harder and harder, punishing her twat. Thinking about what Pavielle had cost him drove him mad and he became lost in his quest for revenge. G-Momma prayed to God inside of her head, seeing as how she couldn't utter the prayer she had in mind. Her eternal walls felt like they had carpet burns on them. She squeezed her eyelids shut and hoped for it all to be over soon. "Unh huh, I bet cho punk ass grandson gon' wish he left this beef alone! This gon' be one beef he gon' wish he left be. 'Cause I'ma do you filthy, you fucking whore! Realllll fucking filthy!" he screamed in her face and specs of spit clung to it as he continued to violate her in the worse way. Unable to take it anymore, her eyelids opened further and she screamed louder and harder. Some of the sound managed to escape this time so he angrily punched her in the jaw, dazing her. Her eyes turned to their whites looking like Q-balls, she groaned in pain. Next, he pulled the blue bandana from his back pocket and stuffed it inside of her grill, pushing it shut and clamping his hand over it. He smiled wickedly and shut his eyelids. His head jumped up and down fast and rapidly as he pumped her without any remorse. Barely conscious, all G-Momma could do was lay there and take the abuse. Feeling himself about to explode, Nightmare pulled out of her and jerked off, shooting his warm jizz on her stretched marked stomach and underneath her chin. When he climbed off of her he was shiny from perspiration and breathing heavily, chest thumping. He used the bandana he'd stuffed into her mouth to wipe his flaccid member off then slipped his Dickies back on. The entire time he was doing this, Taco was staring at him in disgust. He couldn't believe that he'd do such a thing to a defenseless old lady, but now he knew that there were many reasons why the hood had given him the name Nightmare.

"What chu looking at me like that for, Cuz?" the gangsta crip asked, zipping up his Dickies and wiping his wet forehead with the back of his hand. His other hand gripped the banger he'd sat on the table beside G-Momma before he violated her.

"Fuck is the matter witchu? You a fucking monster!" Taco barked, looking at him like he was the devil himself. His brows were lowered and his head was angled to the side.

Nightmare snickered evilly before replying.

"Monster?" he shook his head with his eyelids closed then peeled them back open, "I'm notta monster, lil' homie, I'ma fucking Nightmare…America's Nightmare."

Taco shook his head shamefully. Finally he understood. This was a real life Boogey Man standing before his eyes.

"Yo' turn, Loc." Nightmare spoke as if to say Hey, it's your turn to ride this pony. Using one hand, he stuck a half smoked blunt between his blackened lips and fired it up, a golden glow illuminated the lower half of his face as smoke impregnated the atmosphere surrounding him.

"What?" He lifted an eyebrow and turned up his nose.

Taking the time to pull the blunt from out of his mouth and blow smoke into the air, he responded. "It's yo' turn to run dick up in this old hoe, gon' and get yours, my young nigga. You ain't gotta strap up. Her worn, brittle ass ain't got nothing. That's fa sho' 'cause if she did she wouldn't be alive at what? 70-75?" he looked back at G-Momma who was still lying on the table squirming and moaning her pain.

"Naw," Taco shook his head, repulsed by the thought of doing something so foul to a human being.

"Naw?" the gangsta crip's forehead wrinkled before he took another pull of the blunt, causing smoke to waft all around him.

"Yeah, nigga, naw!" the young nigga snapped. "I'm notta 'bout to do that old ass lady like that! I'm not some... some goddamn savage!" spittle flew from his lips and he jabbed the air with his finger for emphasis.

In a flash, Nightmare's gold burner was up and pointed at his protégé. Seeing the lethal weapon pointed at his chest wiped the tension from Taco's face and drained the hostility from out of him. He couldn't believe that the mothafucka that he loved like a big brother had the balls to draw down on him. Ain't this about a bitch? He thought. Damn, this nigga out here cut throat! We from the same hood, we'pose to be homies.

"Drop the gun, lil' nigga!" he ordered, frowning and blowing smoke out of his nostrils. Taco did like he was told, knowing that his man wouldn't hesitate to leave him soaked wet in that kitchen. "Now, you gon' climb on top of that table and you gon' rape that old skeeza like I said, ya dig?"

Taco glared up at him with his nostrils pulsating and his chest puffing in and out. He didn't say nothing for a time, but when his big homie cocked that hammer on that toy of his, he figured he'd better say something. "Yeah...I dig."

"Good." He shot back. "Now get cho ass over there." He grabbed him by the back of the neck and shoved him over to G-Momma. He held his thang on him and watched as he unzipped and unbuckled his Levi's 501's, taking his time removing them. The entire time he was shooting him with looks that could kill, wishing that he could slice his fucking throat. "Hurry. The. Fuck. Up."

Taco took a deep breath, hating to do what he had been forced to. He climbed onto of the table in between G-momma's legs. He slid up inside of her and squeezed his eyelids shut. Turning his head and feeling disgusted by what he was about to go through with, he began thrusting in and out of her V. Nightmare stood by holding the gun on him and smiling fiendishly, licking his lips. His freehand dipped inside of his Dickies and he began stroking his flaccid penis until it swelled up and its head was throbbing. The veins bulged in his meat as he stroked it slowly then feverishly, causing his eyes to roll because it was feeling so good to him. Pleasure etched across his face hearing G-Momma moan in pain and seeing his little homeboy stoke her through his narrowed eyes. Before long he felt himself about to cum so he turned his dick upward. Grunting, he jerked off, watching the nut ooze out of its head, running over his knuckles. He continued to stroke himself until there wasn't anything left in him. His head snapped up just in time to see Taco pull himself out of G-Momma and jerk himself off on the table, splattering it with his children.

Seeing that his comrade was done, Nightmare snatched off a couple of paper towels from off of the roll and wiped his semen from off of his hand. Once he was all cleaned up, he grabbed a few more paper towels and held them out to Taco. The young nigga snatched them, still pissed at him for making him do that despicable act. Feeling disrespected by what he'd done, Nightmare raised his eyebrow and pointed his gun at him again like Alright now, don't force my hand. Taco wiped off the table and then his hands, mad dogging his big homie. He wanted to pick up his tool and open his chest up with it but they were in a war now and all they had was each other.

"Get that gun outta my face, Cuz, we in this shit together." he told him. "The enemy is out there." He threw his head to the left, referring to the streets were Booby Loco and his goons were watching and waiting for their chance to put both of their asses six feet under.

"That's what I've been tryna tell you, Loc." Nightmare tucked his banger at the small of his back alongside the chrome one he had stored there. His eyes scanned the kitchen until they came across a wooden block of knives. The biggest one of them all had a shiny, metal kilt that twinkled. This brought a wicked smile to his face. When Taco followed his line of vision and saw what he had his sights set on, he bowed his head and massaged the bridge of his nose. He'd gone this far with his main man so he figured he may as well continue to follow him down the road to hell.

Nightmare snatched the biggest knife from out of the block and admired its blade, a gleam swept up its length and its tip twinkled. Whipping around, he approached G-momma and climbed on top of the table, straddling her. He slammed the butcher's knife into her chest and her eyes shot open, making her pupils look smaller than they actually were. Her mouth quivered uncontrollably and she stared at him accusingly. She tried to touch his face but he gritted and smacked her meaty hand down. Madness danced in his eyes and he gritted harder. With a growl, he slammed the knife further into her breast bone, down to its kilt. Blackish blood dribbled over her bottom lip and he curved the blade around the bone, hearing it crackle. His bloody hand continued to make its circle until it reached its beginning. Right after, he was reaching inside of her chest and grasping her beating heart. Taco vomited on the floor seeing him pull her heart out of her center, tearing the valves of it, its dark blood dripping to the linoleum. Droplets splattered on his blue All Star Chuck Taylor's, but he paid it no mind. Letting the stained knife drop to the surface, he approached the wall that you could see as soon as you walked inside of the kitchen.

Using G-momma's heart, Nightmare wrote Pavielle a message in blood. Once he was done, he sat the heart down on the counter and picked up the butcher's knife. He wiped his finger prints off of the murder weapon and tossed it aside. Before he left he grabbed a hold of the kitchen table and flipped it over, spilling Pavielle's grandmother to the floor. Taco stood there looking at the nigga like he was fucking crazy, but he didn't dare utter a word. Passing his little homie as he headed for the door, Nightmare waved him on and he fell in step behind him.

The evil that men do.

***

Pavielle was driving up just in time to see a midnight blue Cadillac bending the corner of Griffith and going down Adams Blvd. His eyes grew big and his lips peeled apart in shock. The kingpin's heart skipped a beat because he knew exactly whose car that was.

"Don't tell me, don't tell me this is happening," Pavielle swallowed the lump of nervousness in his throat as he made a right, driving up into the driveway.

"What's up?" Gouch's forehead crinkled.

"That was him." he unbuckled his safety belt and cocked a copper bullet into the head of his .9mm.

"That was who?" he sat up in his seat, wondering what the hell was going on.

"Nightmare," He threw open the driver side door and hopped out, gun in hand leaving the engine running.

"Oh shit!" Gouch threw open his door and gripped up his Girls, ready to make a nigga go to sleep forever. Pavielle stormed inside of the house with Gouch right on his heels, carrying his twin Berettas. The youngest Hood brother stopped at the center of the living room, head snapping from left to right, gun extended. His eyes were alert as well as his ears.

He called out to his grandmother, "Momma? Momma? Are you alright?" he moved through the house with Gouch by his side, both of his Girls up and pointed, fixed to soak a bitch nigga up. The oldest brother's face was wearing a scowl and his mouth was a straight line. Inside of his head he was expecting the worst, but hoping for the best.

"Maaaa, you still in here?" Gouch called out after his brother.

Pavielle gasped. His eyes turned moist and accumulated with tears, bottom lip quivering. He spotted G-momma lying on her back half naked on the floor in a pool of her own blood. Her eyes were as big as saucers and she was staring past her grandsons.

Pavielle looked up and saw his grandmother's heart on the counter. Above it was a message from Nightmare: You took my heart so I took yours.

"What?" Gouch's forehead furrowed. He looked to his brother having heard him gasp. Seeing him staring ahead at something, he followed his line of vision and found their grandmother dead. His eyes turned glassy as he felt hotness in them, right after his heart sunk into the pit of his stomach. "Ma," he uttered, eyes widening and mouth hanging open. Pavielle was wearing the same expression. However, he quickly snapped out of it and went running towards G-momma. He nearly slipped and fell in her blood, smearing it across the floor. Never minding the blood and getting down on his knees, he sat his tool down on the floor beside him. He pulled his grandmother into his arms and rested her head against his chest. Gouch tucked his bangers on his waistband and pulled off his shirt, draping it over her exposed breasts. Afterwards, he got down on the floor on the opposite side of his brother, taking his grandmother's chubby hand into his, caressing it lovingly. Tears came bursting out of him and his brother's eyes, streaming down their faces. Pavielle wiped his face and sniffled, trying to snort the snot back up his nostrils.

"Oh, God, I beg of you, please, don't let this be happening," Pavielle stared up at the ceiling, exposing beneath his chin, tears encircling his face and trickling to the surface. "Please, don't let her be dead, oh, please, please, please," he pleaded with the Lord Almighty. He couldn't stand the thought of losing the woman that had been like a mother to him. She, Gangsta, and Gouch were the family that he had and to lose any of them would likely cripple him emotionally. Suddenly, he brought his head back down and shut his eyes. Coming to the realization that G-momma was gone and there wasn't anything that he could do about it, he swept long strands of gray hair from out of her face and kissed her forehead tenderly. He then laid the side of his face against the top of her head. Gouch realized that his grandmother was gone, too. Taking G-momma's hand, he rubbed her palm against the side of his face and kissed it. Leaning forward, he kissed her on the cheek and lay down on the floor beside her, wrapping his arms around her and shutting his eyes. He and Pavielle would have their time with their grandmother before they decided to call the police.

Chapter Four

A few days later

At G-momma's funeral Pavielle wore a stone face, but his eyes were glassy and pink, tears falling beneath them. During the repast, he called Gouch into the backyard away from everyone's ears. The oldest of The Hood brothers watched as his sibling paced the ground back and forth like a caged cheetah. Suddenly, he stopped his stride and turned around to face him.

"I want Supa, Nike, Taco and that nigga Nightmare dead, you hear me? Dead, Gucci." Pavielle stared his brother in the face with a pair of pink, moist eyes, tears sprawling down his cheeks. "Call old girl, I want her on homie. I want her on him and I want her on him now."

Gouch nodded and said, "I got chu, I got this." He pounded his fist to his chest, wearing a dead serious expression smeared across his face. He patted his brother on his shoulder and started to walk away, when he grabbed him by the arm. Instinctively, he turned around. Pavielle cupped his face and stared into his eyes.

"He killed, momma, man, he killed ma. Niggaz gotta pay, Gucci. They gotta pay. I want blood."

"Oh, you'll get blood," Gouch assured him, gripping the back of his neck. His eyes had grown glassy thinking of how foul G-momma had been done, "So much blood you can drown in it." He suddenly embraced him, holding on to him for a time before pulling him back and kissing him on the side of the head, "I love you, lil' brother."

"I love you, too." Pavielle embraced him again, sobbing as he held onto him. When they broke their embrace, Pavielle wiped his wet cheeks with the back of his fist. Gouch walked away and pulled out his cellular. It was time to put in some work.

***

"Oh, my God!" Nike's eyelids fluttered and veins formed in his forehead and neck. The light skinned vixen between his legs was sucking his dick so hard she could have vacuumed his soul from out of his body and down her throat. The sensation he was experiencing from her warm, wet mouth sent his form into sensual convulsions. He squirmed under her and walked the sheets straight into the headboard, banging his head up against it. From the look on his face you'd have thought he was transforming into some sort of demonic like creature. "Ahhhh, Cuz, I'ma 'bout to bust! Sssssss." Nike hissed. He went to pull his love muscle from light skin's mouth, but she smacked his hand away and continued to work her magic, gobbiling up that dick. Homegirl was giving Karrine Steffans a run for her title as Superhead inside room #7 of the Eastside Inn.

Nike grabbed the edges of the mattress and pumped his member in and out of her mouth causing slobber to dribble. He went as hard and as fast as he could, trying to reach that nut he so desperately desired. His eyes rolled to the back of his skull and he releasing a shriek that quickly died in his throat as he exploded into light skin's mouth, continuing to hump at her even after he'd gotten off. He eventually collapsed onto the mattress, panting out of breath. Light skin straddled him. She showed him the semen cupped in her tongue before swallow-ing it and licking her lips.

"Mmmmm," She smiled at him and sucked her fingers as if his cum was delicious.

"Oh, no you didn't, you nasty mothafucka," Nike continu-ously panted as he stared down at homegirl. He was surprised that she had swallowed his children. Oh, my fucking God, I love this bitch, he thought.

"Are you ready for round two?" She asked between the kisses she planted up Nike's chest and neck.

"Oh, you know it, baby," Nike grinned as his chest rose and fell, occasionally his form jerked feeling the after effects of that nut he'd let off in her mouth. "I think I'ma need another head start though, if you know what I'm saying." He smiled broadly, raising and dropping his eyebrows rapidly.

"I got chu, boo. You just lay back, close your eyes, and let the pleasure train take you away." She eyed him seductively and stuck her manicured finger into his mouth, watching him suck it attentively.

Nike closed his eyelids and licked his lips as light skin brought her head up and down his length, returning him to a utopia of pleasure he'd not too long ago left. He was happy he had stopped and helped little momma with her car when it had stalled. At first he wasn't going to since his hood was beefing with the bloods so hard but after the blow job she'd given him he was glad that he did.

China Doll stared up at Nike as she blessed him with one of her many talents. She slowly pulled out the needles that held her hair in place in a bun, letting it fall loose. With lightning fast reflexes, she struck the pressure points in her victim's legs and right-arm, paralyzing him. She was just about to jab the needle into his left-arm when he backhanded her with his fist, knocking her to the floor. While she lay there he desperately tried to reach the banger that lay beside him on the dresser. He struggled and strained trying to reach it, and he'd just gotten it in his palm when the femme fatal jabbed him in the forearm with a needle paralyzing his left-arm. She then picked herself up from the floor and cracked him in the jaw, bloodying his mouth.

Nike spat a slither of blood on the floor and roared, "You high yellow bitch, I'ma cut your fucking titties off!"

China Doll paid Nike no mind as she carried her tattooed form across the room, ass cheeks jiggling one at a time. Her body was nearly completely covered in Chinese artwork. It looked as if she was wearing a bodysuit. Only her hands, breasts, and feet were visible. She wrapped herself in a kimono and opened the door. When Nike saw Pavielle and Killa Dre stroll into the motel, his eyes doubled and his heart quickened. Although Pavielle appeared to be calm and solemn, Killa Dre wore a mask of murder.

"Good looking out, sis," Pavielle told China Doll.

"Don't mention it, Booby. You know a bitch got cha back." She handed him Nike's gun and pecked him on the cheek sweetly.

"What's up, crab?" Pavielle smiled at Nike. "What's that Rolling 20s Bloods Gang like, homeboy?"

"I wouldn't know, Loc. I'ma Eastside Crip until they bury me." The hardhead sneered defiantly, refusing to show fear in the face of death.

"That might be pretty soon if you don't tell me what I wanna know." Pavielle spoke from the heart. He had ever intention on killing that lil' mothafucka if he didn't tell him what he wanted to know. "We know it was you and Supacrab that smoked the homie Panic, but what we wanna know is who laid down lil' Tramel Johnson?"

"Yeah, Blood, tell us who the fuck smoked my big brother?" Killa Dre's face was twisted in a mad dog glare.

"Cuz, do you know how many niggaz the set done twisted? What makes this lil' mothafucka so special that he's supposed to stand out in my mind?" Nike asked, his evil eyes staring up at Killa Dre.

Killa Dre took a deep breath and recounted his brother's murder that night. When he finished telling the story, his eyes had become glassy. Although he wanted to let the tears fall, there was no way hell he was going to give the nigga strapped to the bed the satisfaction of knowing what his hood had done had affected him in such a way. Nah, he would never do that. He was going to handle his like the G he was.

"Awwww, don't tell me you're going to cry." Nike gave him sadden eyes and a pouty lip, looking like a sad ass puppy.

"Fuck you!"

"Fuck you too, nigga!" Nike laughed. He sucked the blood from his teeth and swallowed it. "Yeahhhh, I remember now," He nodded, grinning and looking sinister. "The homie Reboc did tell us about smoking your bitch ass brother, may he rest in shit." He harped up phlegm and spat it across the room. It splattered against Killa Dre's sneaker. He then went on to tell him how his brother and a host of others were murdered out by his homeboy. The vindictive mothafucka gave them the story in detail just as Reboc had given it to him and Suparip, leaving nothing out. After hearing this, Pavielle and Killa Dre clenched their jaws and balled their fists tightly. They were hot as fire crackers and ready to put a hurting on him. "But trip off of this shit, Cuz, had it been me I would have tortured his lil' punk ass before I let him meet with death, ya feel me?" he said coldheartedly. "Peep this, the coldest part about it was my nigga Reboc was out there tripping hard 'cause he was high and looking to bust on some fools that murdered out his brother. But the nigga that had done it was right under his nose. Who you ask? Nightmare," He threw his head back laughing maniacally, showcasing all of his cavities and his tongue. Tears of humor accumulated in his eyes and rolled freely.

"You bitch ass nigga," Killa Dre spat heatedly. He moved to do Nike harm, but Pavielle blocked him by bringing his arm across his chest.

"Where's Reboc and Nightmare?" Pavielle scowled.

"Nigga, what?" Nike looked at him like he was fucking crazy, the remnants from his tears of laughter still in his eyes. "Fuck you think I am? I'm not telling y'all niggaz shit else. Suck my mothafucking dick…bitch! If you're going to kill me, then kill me! I don't give a fuck! I'm a still be from Gangstas." He tilted his head down, glaring up at them, sneering like an angry dog poised to attack.

"Killa," Pavielle called out to his little homie without taking his eyes off of Nike. He tried to hand the gun to him but he refused it. With a flick of his wrist, Killa Dre triggered the blade of his switchblade and moved in on the mouthy crip. He straddled him and stuffed his mouth with a red bandana. Holding Nike's jaws tight with one hand, he proceeded to carve his eyes out of their sockets. Nike tried to shriek but the sound was blocked by the gag. China Doll and Pavielle stood by watching the entire thing without so much as batting an eye. They were pleased to see one of their enemies get what he deserved.

Killa Dre pulled the gag from Nike's mouth and clutched his bottom jaw so tight with his bloody hand that his grill stayed stuck open. Wearing a concentrated expression across his face, he proceeded to carve the bad ass crip's tongue out. His empty eye sockets were black orbs and running streams of blood. The young nigga stared down at victim as he clean off his bed on the bed sheet and stashed it back inside of his pocket. Nike looked like something out of a horror movie with his eyes and tongue missing.

With the deed done, Killa Dre fished around in Nike's pants pocket until he produced a cell phone.

Scrolling through the text messages, he found a message that brought a smiled to his face. "I found the address, I know where he's at?" he told Pavielle who'd just reentered to the room with a gas-can.

"Let me see that," Pavielle took the cell phone from Killa Dre.

"Where's China?" the young nigga's forehead crinkled.

"Waiting in the car," The kingpin snapped pictures of Nike's mutilated body.

"Fuck you doing, Blood?" he looked from the dead form to his homeboy.

"You'll see." He sent out picture messages of what he'd just taken snaps of.

***

Nightmare lay in bed watching TV inside of his hotel room. He and Bobby had taken up space at this suite after Booby and his people hit his spot and murdered Karma. As of now he was relaxing and mentally preparing for his next move. Just when he had formulated his next move, his cell phone violently shook on the nightstand ringing. At first he wasn't going to answer it, but he remembered he had tried to contact his connect earlier that night for some more work. Nightmare picked up his cell and saw that he had six picture messages. When he looked through the pictures of Nike's mutilated corpse, his facial expression slowly changed to one of great sadness and pain. He reached the last picture and it was a close up of Nike's bloody face. The caption read You're next. This sent a chill up the gangster crip's spine, and he shook Bobby Blue awake.

What happened, baby? What's wrong?" Bobby asked wincing, sitting up in bed and wiping her eyes.

"Get the fuck up, we getting outta here!" Nightmare sneered, stepping into his Dickies hurriedly.

"Why, what's going on?" she worried.

"Bitch, I don't have time to explain. Get up!" He barked as he zipped up his pants.

Meanwhile

Detectives Arsenegger and Ortiz stood looking over three pyramids of pictures on the white board. The first pyramid was of Black Jesus and the members of his organization, the second was Gangsta's, the third was Pavielle's, and the last one was Nightmare's. The men who were dead in the four organizations pictures were marked with a red X.

"Looks like these guys are doing our dirty work for us," Aresengger looked between Nightmare's pyramid and Pavielle's. They both had a significant amount of soldiers whose pictures were crossed out. "Good. We'll let them, and then we'll clean the rest of these shit-birds up once the smoke has cleared."

"Then we'll focus on the homes here," Ortiz circled Black Jesus' picture. "And then this prick," He circled Tango's picture. "He's been operating under the D.E.A's nose for years using his bodyguard services as a front while moving weight; nothing too major, but enough to be on the radar. He's making moves, and from what my source tells me he's forming an empire of his own, one that'll rival Black Jesus'."

"I don't think that's going to sit too well with god's son." Arsenegger twisted the cap off of his bottle water and took a drink.

"Are you kidding? If the guy knew he'd probably kill him."

"Oh, I don't doubt that." Aresenegger replied. "How many of the guys are with us on our thing?"

"Including you and myself? Eight," Ortiz told him.

"Not an impressive number, but we'll have to make due; best to have someone watching our backs than no one at all."

Chapter 5

The next day

Three months ago Bully and Thangz had moved out of her aunt's house and into his grandma's basement. Their stay was supposed to have been temporary until they found an apartment for rent, but Bully had gotten sprung out on crack so bad that he and Thangz ended up staying.

Bully had blown through the money Pavielle had given him as well as his own stash. He sold his jewelry, his flatscreen, the furniture and the home appliances he had bought for their apartment. It all had to be sacrificed to feed the monkey on his back. The only thing he had of value was his whip, and he had even sold the chrome rims off of that.

As of now the crack head couple lay on the mattress in his grandma's basement as high as the moon. Bully's cell phone rung and he picked it up. Seeing that it was Pavielle on the screen made him sober up quickly. He pressed talk and brought the cellular to his ear.

"Hello?" he spoke into his device.

"What it two, O.G?" Pavielle asked.

"Aint shit, bicking back being bool," He replied. "How you been, though?"

"I'm good," He answered, "Chasing this bread."

"I heard that, family." Bully paused for a moment. "So, is this a social call?"

"Straight to the point, huh?" Pavielle smirked. "I know you said you were done with Booby's pizzeria, but I've got a few deliveries I need to get out there. And I need a delivery boy. You down? It pays well." He spoke in a code that he knew he'd understand.

"I could use the extra chips," Bully massaged his chin as he thought on it. He knew Pavielle was talking about delivering work for a salary, and he didn't have a problem with it. He could make a few runs and have some more money to cop crack with. "Fuck it. Where and when you tryna meet?"

"Shit now, I'm at the Bat Cave," Pavielle informed him. The Bat-Cave was code for the trap house on 23rd and San Pedro.

"Gimmie thirty minutes."

"Bool," Pavielle replied, "Two hundred."

He hung up.

***

"Who was that?" Thangz asked, taking a pull from the crack pipe.

"Booby Loco," Bully said, picking himself up from the mattress. "I gotta make this run for him real quick, and I need you to roll, so dress in something formal."

Thangz blew smoke into the air before saying, "Oh, we're back fucking with Booby now?"

"You wanna get high, don't chu?" he asked with a raised eyebrow.

"Hell yeah, I wanna get high!"

"Well, get your ass up then!"

When Black Jesus informed Pavielle that his usual shipment wouldn't be in until next month, he was glad that he copped sixty bricks instead of his usual thirty when he re-up'd the last time. The weight he had should last him until Black Jesus' shipment came through next month. His problem now was distribution. Since the war broke out seeing a crack head was as rare as seeing a pregnant midget. His main clientele now was the hustlers outside of The Bottoms. They wouldn't come through the hood to cop from him for fear of getting caught up in the crossfire from the beef, so he would deliver to them with a sales tax tacked on the principal. The hustlers didn't mind the tax because Pavielle's product was all of that and a bag of chips.

Forty five minutes later

Bully pulled up at the trap house on 23rd and San Pedro. He hopped out of the whip and made his way over to Pavielle and Gouch, who were posted in the driveway.

"What's up, my niggaz?" Bully raised his fist to give Pavielle a pound, but he left him hanging. He was looking over Bully's shoulder at Thangz in the passenger seat of his ride.

"Hey, Booby," Thangz waved like a beauty pageant contestant. Her smile showcased her missing, decaying teeth.

"Blood, what the fuck is your problem bringing this bitch here?" Pavielle sneered.

"Aye, watch cho mouth, nigga, that's my lady." He balled up his face, looking at him like he was crazy for mention his woman in such a way.

Pavielle scowled, veins pulsating at his temples he was so angry. "You putting a crack whore in my business, jeopardizing what I've got going, risking me and my mothafucking peoples going to the pen!" he spat, smacking the back of his hand in his palm as he emphasized.

"Hold up, Booby, Blood!" Bully snapped. "Remember who the fuck you're talking to! I'm your big homie! It's not the other way around! Show me the mothafucking proper respect, family! I thought bringing Thangz along would make me seem incognito. Both of us dressed casually as If we're going to church or some shit. Binem see that and it would throw them off. They wouldn't think twice about stopping us. I'm thinking ahead." He tapped his finger against his temple.

Pavielle had stopped listening to Bully after he had said 'Show me the mothafucking proper respect'. He was too busy taking in his appearance. See, Bully had lost a significant amount of weight since he last saw him, fifty pounds to be exact. His muscles looked as if they were melting. His eyes were sunken in with black rings around them and his face was ashy. His appearance coupled with the button-down shirt and tie he was wearing made him look like a dead man who dug himself up out of the ground.

"Blood, are you back smoking again?" Pavielle's forehead indented and his eyebrows dipped low.

"What? Hell nah!" Bully lied, looking guilty as shit. "I don't fuck with that shit no more!"

"Nigga, do I look like a mothafucking fool to you?" Pavielle went off heatedly. "I'm supplying the shit, dummy! I think I should know what it does to niggaz out here!" he looked him up and down and then shook his head shamefully. "My big homie ain't nothing but a mothafucking smoker, Blood."

Pavielle's last statement struck a chord within Bully, and he snarled and swung on him. The young kingpin side stepped him, and he went stumbling forward. The O.G caught himself and got into a boxer's stance. He tucked his chin to his chest and moved in on Pavielle, throwing a combination of punches. The younger man was a lot faster than his opponent; his movements were fluid as he dodged the assault. Bully was huffing and puffing; all the crack he had smoked these past few months was making him pay with interest.

Gouch stood by smiling wickedly and rubbing his hands together. He loved a good fight. There was nothing more amusing to him than a ghetto brawl.

"What the fuck is going on, Gucci?" Thangz hollered out from the car, stepping out onto the sidewalk one sandaled, ashy foot at a time.

"A mothafucking squabble," he answered, not bothering to take his eyes off of the action.

"Well, stop 'em!" she pleaded, looking between him and the fight.

"Nah, fuck that! They're grown men. Let 'em do what they do." He scrunched his face up as he continued watching the brawl, imitating his baby brother throwing the punches.

Pavielle and Bully circled each other like two wild pit bulls in an arena. The older gangsta threw a punch that grazed the younger man's shoulder when he went to bob it. When his head came back up Bully landed a solid over hand right dead in his mouth, bloodying his teeth. The blow split Pavielle's bottom lip and woke him up, he shook off his daze. But before he could counter, a punch to the chin sat him on his ass. He sat there for a minute trying to gather his wits; it took three tries before he was back on his feet.

"That's right, baby, fuck that nigga up! Kick his ass!" Thangz cheered Bully on and threw phantom punches.

"Come on, baby bro, you can take this old ass nigga." Gouch said loud enough for only him to hear.

Pavielle licked his busted lip as he got back into a fighting stance, ready to get it in. Bully rushed in throwing hooks that would of tore his head off if they would have connected. The young kingpin stepped back for a breather after evading the assault; he sized his opponent up and stepped back in. He threw a series of jabs and punches that buckled his opponent. Dazed, Bully threw a couple of weak jabs that couldn't break wind.

"Yeah, that's what I'm talking about, baby," Gouch clapped his hands like a spectator at a heavy weight champion fight. "Gone and finish him off, bro."

Pavielle threw an uppercut that laid Bully flat on his back. "You gone come on my mothafucking property and start this bullshit, nigga?" he spat on an unconscious Bully as he lay sprawled on the surface. He then started kicking and stomping him, busting up his face and mouth.

"Oh, hell nah," Thangz shouted as she popped the trunk of her man's ride and withdrew a baseball bat. She slammed the trunk shut and rushed up the driveway. Before she could reach Pavielle, his big brother stepped in her path and drew his banger.

"Bitch, who you plan on hitting with that bat?" Gouch sneered with threatening eyes. "If you know like I know, you better drop that mothafucka like its hot!" Thangz' eyes shot open and her mouth fell open. She dropped the baseball bat and put her hands up, shivering. "Yeah, that's what I thought; now go pick that bum ass nigga up and get 'em outta here 'fore I catch a couple hommies out this bitch!"

Pavielle stepped to the side and allowed Thangz to help Bully to his feet. As she turned to walk him down the driveway, she shot him and his brother a deadly look.

Pavielle and Gouch watched as Thangz loaded Bully into the car.

"You should have smoked that fool, Booby," Gouch told his baby brother as they watched the whip disappear down the block.

"Nah, we're not going to have to worry about blood no more, he knows better." Pavielle assured him.

Little did he know he'd live to regret those words.

Chapter 6

Reboc sat before a 42 inch flat-screen playing *Fight Night* on PS4 with Lil' Dontai. The scrawny, brown skinned kid was beating the living shit out of his ass, but the gangbanging veteran didn't care. He had gotten a text earlier from Nike that said he was sending a car to get him to bring him back to the hood. Nightmare had his hands full with the war back home and he needed every able body he could get.

Drama was right up Reboc's alley. He had been cooped up in Nightmare's sister's apartment for the last couple of weeks. He had been confined there so long that he started to feel institutionalized, but he had to suffer through it. He was advised by Nightmare to lay low after he had caught a body. He was reluctant to do so, but when that crazy mothafucka advises you to do something you had better do it.

Reboc was excited. He couldn't wait to get back home and be in the mix of all the bullshit. So he didn't mind getting his ass handed to him by a seven year old.

"Boom! Boom! Boom!" Lil' Dontai said as his character delivered a three punch combination that laid Reboc's character on his back. He hopped up from the couch and counted the numbers the referee shouted as they appeared on the screen. "One, two, three, four, five…" Reboc rose to his feet punching the buttons furiously, trying to get his character back on his feet. The countdown continued on the screen with Lil' Dontai calling them out loud. "Six, seven, eight, nine…" Reboc clenched his jaws as he rapidly punched the buttons, desperately trying to make his character get back up on its feet. "Ten!" Lil' Dontai shouted, spiking his controller like a football. He jumped in Reboc's face talking big shit. The Eastside Crip balled up in the corner of the couch, laughing his ass off.

"Dontai!" a voice yelled from the doorway of one of the bedrooms. "Boy, get off Reboc, have you lost your mind?"

Big Dontai entered the living room taking pulls from a Sess blunt. He walked over to the couch and plopped down beside his son. Big Dontai was a reputable Blood from Black P Stones, who went by the name Tay-Rock. It was because of him that Reboc got to stay within The Jungle without some knucklehead putting heat to him.

"What's up, my nigga?" Big Dontai asked Reboc.

"What up?" Reboc responded.

"I see junior in here tapping that ass in Fight Night," Big Dontai ruffled his son's head.

"Yep, I was kicking his butt." His mini me chimed in.

"Yeah, lil' dude got me, but I'll get'em next time, though." Reboc gave him a half hearted smile. He wasn't too fond of Big Dontai. To him he wasn't a man. All he did was eat, sleep and shit while Nightmare's sister worked, took care of home, and their son. The nigga was a bum to the tenth power, but that wasn't any of his business though. He was just there to lay low until things blew over, so he was going to keep his mouth shut.

Big Dontai took a few more pulls of his blunt and then blew the smoke into the air. The smoke made his son gag and fan the smoke away.

"Wanna hit this?" Big Donai asked Reboc as he held out the blunt.

Reboc frowned at the stench of the burning blunt held out before him. "Fuck is that shit?" he asked disgusted, face balled up.

"Sess, my nigga; shit bomb." He replied, holding the smoke in his lungs.

Reboc looked at him as if he had just offered him a blow-job. "Man, I don't fuck with that shit, its Kush or nothing."

"More for me," Big Dontai shrugged his shoulders and continued to smoke his blunt.

Boom!

A spray of debris and splinters flew everywhere as the front door was blown open by a powerful kick. Two men rushed inside wearing ski-masks and clutching pistol grip pumps. Reboc dropped the PS4 controller and threw his hands up in the air, while Lil' Dontai cowered at the corner of the couch. Dontai jumped to his feet and darted towards the bedroom to retrieve his banger. He got about four feet before a blast spun him back around and a second slammed him up against the wall, decorating it with a crimson splatter. He slid down to the floor, slumped with his head hung and his palms up.

"Daddyyyyyyyy," Lil' Dontai screamed as he ran towards his father, tears spilling from the corners of his eyes. Before he could reach his father, the tallest of the ski-masked men grabbed him from behind and clamped his gloved hand over his mouth. Lil' Dontai flailed his scrawny arms trying to break free, but he was no match for the strength of a grown ass man.

When Reboc saw Dontai go down he closed his eyes and shook his head. He peeled his eyes open to find himself being eclipsed by the shadow of the shorter of the ski-masked men. Reboc put up the meanest mug he could muster and then looked up into the shorter man's eyes. He already knew that he wouldn't be living past that night, so he decided he was going to go out like the beast the streets claimed him to be. He harped up some phlegm and spat it on the shorter man's sneaker and smiled wickedly.

The shorter masked man looked from the yellowish goo on his sneaker to the wicked smile on Reboc's face. He pressed his pistol grip pump into his brother's murderer's palm. Before Reboc could snatch his hand away half of it was being blown off, blood and mutilated fingers shot across the living room. All that was left of Reboc's hand was a bloody thumb and stump. His eyes bulged and his mouth stretched open as far as it could as he screamed at the top of his lungs. He tucked what was left of his hand under his armpit and fell off the couch and onto the floor, bawling in agony.

"I bet chu see now what all that rah rah shit get chu, huh?" The short masked man kneeled down to a grimacing Reboc. He pulled the ski-mask off and Reboc looked into his face. He ran his face through his mental database but couldn't find a name to match it. He hadn't a clue as to who he was.

"Yo, Blood, what the fuck are you doing?" the tallest of the masked men asked. This was Gouch. He was still holding a squirming Lil'Dontai.

Killa Dre threw up a hand, calling for his homeboy's silence.

"That kid you shot down in the street as if he were nothing was my big brother, Tramel Johnson." Killa Dre spoke behind bloodshot eyes as tears slicked his cheeks wet. His talking was cool and calm, yet displayed the hurt and anger in his heart.

"So, fuck that nigga, you think I care?" Reboc hollered back into Killa Dre's face, spit flying from off his lips.

"Nope, but here's something you may care about," Killa Dre began, "Your lil' brotha Dizzy, Nightmare murked 'em. Why? Die wondering, mothafucka." He pressed the pump under Reboc's chin and pulled the trigger. Killa Dre shut his eyes just as blood smacked against his face. He rose to his feet wiping his face with the sleeve of his shirt. He kneeled down to little nigga and motioned for his partner to release him. Lil' Dontai mad dogged Killa Dre as tears cascaded down his cheeks. He was so angry that Killa Dre could feel the heat radiating from him. The little boy wanted to kill him, but fear of being murdered before he could get revenge stayed his hand.

"Sorry about cha daddy lying over there," Killa Dre threw his head towards Dontai's dead body, "I'll chalk up his murder as a necessary evil. Seeing as how he was a loved one I'm sure his death has left you in your feelings, so when you grow up…if you still feel some type of way about it…I want chu to come see me. We'll settle up then."

Killa Dre and Gouch walked towards the door. They'd just about crossed the threshold when Lil Dontai spoke.

"When I get bigger, I'm find you and I'ma smoke your ass." Tears streamed down the little nigga'z face and his nostrils flared, standing there tight lipped.

Killa Dre turned around to Lil' Dontai. The little boy was giving him the evil eye and sneering at him.

"I'm counting on it, lil' soldier," Killa Dre and Gouch continued out of the door.

***

Nightmare stood on the balcony of his hotel room taking sips of Jack as he over looked the city. At night Los Angeles was the most beautiful city he'd ever seen. Its mesh of colorful lights set against the ebony backdrop made it look like Las Vegas. A day ago Nightmare's world had been turned upside down. He received a picture text of Nike with gaping holes where his eyes used to be. Right after, his cellular was ringing off the hook with the homies saying they had received the same text.

Nightmare knew that Pavielle's hands were stained with Nike's blood. He might not have pulled the trigger himself, but he for sure gave the go ahead. The young kingpin was trying to draw him out with hopes of killing him. The gangster crip was too smart to fall for that little strategy though. The shit was chess not checkers, so he knew his next move had to be his best move.

Nightmare threw back the last of his Jack and headed back inside.

Meanwhile

Killa Dre sat on the roof of his house punishing a clear plastic cup of Gin mixed with orange juice. He stared up into the stars. He believed beyond them there was a heaven, and in that heaven his brother's soul rested.

The young nigga was drunk as a skunk and his eyes were glassy and red webbed. "I got that pussy for you, Mel. You can finally rest in peace, big bro." he took a swallow and hissed as the liquor burned his throat, its hot bath engulfing his stomach with flames. "I'm a hold it down on this earth 'til my number's called. So until then, you save me a spot up there, alright? I love you, my nigga. Salute," He saluted the sky with the Blood gang sign and climbed down from the roof of the house. He walked off taking the occasional swig of his alcohol beverage.

Finally his big brother Tramel could rest in peace.

Chapter 7

Fat Travon, his cousin and his homeboy ate outside of Tam's on 28th and Central. The beating Pavielle and Gouch had administered left the chubby hustler a gimp. He was forsaken to walk the scandalous streets of South Central with a cane the rest of his life.

"Let me get this straight," Travon began, wiping his mouth and balling up the napkin. "You're telling me that Jackie Chan can whoop Bruce Lee's ass? Come on now. You haven't seen The Game of Death or Enter the Dragon, have you?"

"Yeah, yeah, yeah, The Game of Death, Enter the Dragon, The Big Boss. I've seen them all." One of his homeboys waved him off. There were three of them sitting at the table, Travon included. "Jackie Chan does his own stunts; does Bruce Lee do his own stunts?"

"Blood, what the fuck does that have to do with it?" Travon asked before stuffing his mouth full of chili cheese fries.

"What's up witchu, Damu?" a voice asked from the darkness. Travon turned around and Bully stepped into the light illuminating over the outside tables. The rays quickly filled out his features and physique. He was taking pulls from a withering cigarette. The smoke coming from it whipped around him like tentacles and evaporated in the air.

"What's up, Blood?" Travon threw his head back like *What's up?* Then wiped his mouth and hands with a napkin. He was a little tense being aware of Bully's reputation as a jacker and killer. The two of them hadn't shared so much as two words since he came home, so he wondered what his intentions were. For all he knew Pavielle had sent him to finish what he started on Adams.

"Just came to talk, so you can tell your goons to chill." Bully told him. Through his peripherals he spotted the two men at the table creeping towards the bangers stashed in their waistbands.

Travon raised his hand, staying his goons. "Now, what do you and I have to talk about?" he asked, picking up his soft drink and taking a sip from the straw.

"O.G Booby Loco. I think it's time his reign ended," Bully expelled smoke from his nostrils.

A sinister smile stretched across Travon's face showcasing his bottom row of bunched up teeth. The O.G was talking that shit that he wanted to hear.

"I couldn't agree more with you."

***

Pavielle and Gouch sat at the kitchen table running cash through money-machines and separating them into ten thousand dollar stacks. There were ten cardboard boxes surrounding the brothers' feet, all of which were loaded with dead presidents.

Debo, Woo, and Big Head stood around with assault rifles and machineguns. They were there to hold down the fort in case any knuckleheads tried to kick the door down and stick the trap up.

"Blood, I can't believe that nigga Bully back smoking." Big Head took a pull of his Newport.

"Believe it. 'cause that nigga'z far gone off that shit." Pavielle loaded another stack of cash into the machine.

"How the mighty have fallen. When I was locked up in juvie I heard all kinds of stories about the homie. That nigga'z gangster is well respected."

"Yeah, Blood, is a legend." Woo added his two cents as he ate sunflower seeds.

"But being a smoker gone tarnish his rep," Big Head said.

"Nah, the only thing that would tarnish homie's rep was if he was to turn snitch, and we all know that isn't going to happen." Gouch put a rubber band around a stack of money. "Nothing can change what he did out here in these streets. His resume is etched in stone with a sheet of Teflon laid over that mothafucka. Bully is a straight up killer. All niggaz like him respect is a body, which is why I don't understand why dumb ass didn't let me put that old dog down when I had the chance." He cut his eyes at Pavielle, who had twisted his lips and waved him off.

"Gouch is right, Blood, you should have let'em smoke that fool." Debo told Pavielle from where he was perched in his wheelchair. About five years ago a couple of niggaz in ski-masks had raided his crib looking for a come up. When they didn't find little more than a couple bands they left him with a gift: a .45 caliber slug in the back. That was alright though, because the homies had caught up with them fools and made them pay the ultimate price: death. "Bully is a killer. Now, we done all put in our fair share of work, but that nigga is the best there is at what we do. You Griff me? You done shot homeboy and you whipped his ass in front of his bitch. How much humiliation do you think that man is gone take?"

Pavielle nodded his head as he stared at nothing in particular. Debo made a valid point; maybe he should have let Gouch lay Bully down. He didn't want to go day to day looking over his shoulder.

"Blood, mothafuck Bully," Big Head laughed as he gave Woo a pound. The whole kitchen erupted into laughter. All of the homies were talking shit and horsing around.

***

Gouch, Pavielle and Debo loaded the boxes into two separate vans while Woo and Big Head posted out front as lookouts. A Ford Explorer coasted by as if its driver was looking for an address. Woo and Big Head wrapped their fingers around the triggers of their weapons and were ready to squeeze at the first sign of trouble.

Boof! Sssss!

The van Pavielle and Gouch were in caught a flat.

"Bitches and hoes," Gouch cursed, looking back at the flat tire from behind the wheel. "Goddamn!" he fumed, pulling the van over onto the lawn.

"What's up?" Debo asked.

"Mothafucking flat," Gouch answered angrily. He and Pavielle hopped out of the van and made their way around back to retrieve the spare tire and the jack.

Blatatatatatatatatatatatat!

Suddenly, automatic gunfire erupted, startling Debo, Gouch and Pavielle. Drawing their weapons and taking cover, they looked around and found Woo and Big Head dumping on a Ford Explorer carrying four masked shooters. The three men joined the fray and turned the fury of their weapons on the SUV alongside their comrades, lighting shit up. The flames flickering from their weapons barrels illuminated their scowling faces.

Spent shell-casings dropped on both sides and before long Woo and Big Head were chewed up by missile shaped bullets. Their blood sprayed the crisp, cold air as they collapsed where they stood. "Nooooo," Pavielle shouted seeing his comrades bite the dust. He drew a bead on the Explorer's front wheel tire as it rolled past. He closed his left-eye and pulled the trigger, gun jerking. The tire exploded. The driver lost control of the truck and it crashed into a parked pick-up truck.

There was a moment's silence as both sides ejected the spent magazines from their weapons and loaded new ones. The driver of the Explorer tried to turn the engine over but it was no use. So he hopped out and laid down some cover fire for his escape. Pavielle took a couple of shots at him, but once the rest of the shooters spilled from the Explorer, he went to aid Debo and Gouch. With their combined efforts the three men were able to ground two of the shooters. After running out of ammo, the last shooter tossed his machinegun and made a run for it. He got about five feet before a sweep of Debo's M-16 laid him down.

"Arrrrrrrr!" his victim flailed to the ground.

"Got that mothafucka!" Debo announced, laying his assault rifle across his lap and wheeling toward the curb. "Come on y'all." He waved Pavielle and Gouch on as he rolled out into the street. "Turn your hoe ass over, nigga!" he spat, slamming the butt of his weapon in his ribs. The wounded man howled in pain as he rolled over on his back.

"It's me, Debo! Don't kill me, Blood, don't kill me!" the wounded man pleaded, wincing. Pavielle, Debo and Gouch frowned and exchanged glances. The voice they heard sounded familiar to them.

Gouch peeled the ski-mask off of the man's face. It was Fat Travon. "Who the fuck would have thought?" He couldn't believe who was lying before his eyes.

Pavielle harped up phlegm and spat it on Travon's face, it splattered against his cheek. "Piece of shit!" he stomped his mothafucking nuts.

Travon's eyes bulged and his mouth stretched wide open, as he grabbed his aching balls. "Awwwww!" he blared like an alarm, his tongue vibrating inside of his mouth.

"Who the fuck was the driver, nigga?" Debo asked, leaning over in his chair with his M-16 pointed at his victim's face. The stock of his weapon was braced against his shoulder and his left-eye was shut, peering down at the sighting at its barrel. He was ready to blow this nigga'z cabbage to leaves.

Scarface's Never seen a man cry played in Pavielle's head as he watched Travon cry and cough up blood. The young kingpin tapped Debo and gave him a nod before starting back in the way he'd came, gun held at his side. With Pavielle out of his sight, the wheelchair bound killer focused his attention back on the nigga leaking out into the street.

Travon whimpered like a little bitch, tears rolling down his cheeks. "Bully, man, you've gotta get me to a hospital!"

"I don't know about the hospital, homeboy," Debo placed the barrel of his M-16 into Travon's mouth, causing him to gag. "But I can get chu to the morgue." He spoke coldheartedly.

Walking back towards the house, Pavielle heard the gunshot that ended another one of his enemy's lives.

Blat!

***

Woo and Big Head's funeral took place on a Sunday afternoon. Everybody from the hood turned out. Pavielle wore an all black tailored suit from Calogero's, substituting the white handkerchief for a red bandana. Gouch donned a red brim and a red silk shirt.

As the fat, balding minister patted his sweaty forehead with his handkerchief and gave a sermon about the ills of revenge and how precious life was, Ms. Brown and Mrs. Clark, Woo and Big Head's mothers, stood wrapped in each other's arms, crying their eyes out.

Woo and Big Head were best friends since kindergarten. They hung together so much that people thought they were brothers. They spent so much time at one another's homes that their mothers adopted each other's sons. So when the boys were murdered, it was like the mothers had lost two sons instead of one.

"Damn, Ms. Clark taking Big Head's death hard," Gouch whispered into Pavielle's ear.

"Shit, Big Head was her only son." Pavielle told him.

"Man, shit's fucked up." Gouch shook his head like it was a crying shame.

Pavielle stared straight ahead at nothing in particular, allowing his mind to wander. He vowed to himself that if a nigga was to take Vayda and the baby away from him that he would pry open the gates of hell and unleash it on earth.

"Booby, Booby!" Neck Bone snapped his fingers and waved his hand before Pavielle's eyes. "Is anybody home?"

"Huh?" Pavielle snapped out of his day dream. "Oh, what's up?" he blinked his eyes like he was waking up from a dream.

"I was saying, don't worry about old boy, me and Ridah Man gone take care of that. If you know what I mean." He made his hand into the shape of a gun and pulled an imaginary trigger.

"You sure y'all got this?" Pavielle gave him a pound.

"Don't worry about nothing, dawg, we got this." Neck Bone assured him, dead serious look in his eyes.

Chapter 8

Bully looked both ways before jogging across the street from the trap house. He hopped into the car where Thangz eagerly awaited him and slammed the door closed. He turned around to her with three nickel rocks in his palm. She looked from the rocks to him and then back again.

"Is that all?" she asked with a raised eyebrow, disappointed.

"Fuck you mean is that all?" Bully snapped, twisting his face. She had some fucking nerves. "Bitch, you've been smoking good and plenty these past few months. On my dollar, I may add. And you got the audacity to turn your nose up?" Thangz just stared at the three pebbles of crack in Bully's dry, ashy palm. "Fuck it, more for me." He said. Before he could close his palm, Thangz snatched one of the rocks and grabbed one of the scarred, glass pipes from the ashtray. "Fucking crackhead." He shook his head, watching her light up.

"Nigga, I ain't no crackhead," She snaked her neck with attitude. "If I'ma crackhead, then ya momma's a mothafucking crackhead, alright?"

"Whatever, bitch, you smoke more than I do." Bully claimed as he took the other crack pipe from the ashtray. After depositing crack inside of it, he lit up the pipe and took a long pull. As soon as he blew smoke a cherry red Kawasaki Ninja motorcycle zipped passed him, its engine squealing loudly. He looked out his side view mirror and saw two black leather clad men wearing helmets on the bike. *Fucking fags,* he thought as he shook his head, seeing the man on the back of the motorcycle hanging on like he was some broad. Bully was about to hit the pipe again when the Ninja came blowing past him on the sidewalk.

"What the hell is wrong with these fools?" Thangz asked annoyed, scrunching up her nose.

"I don't know but these mothafuckaz are ruining my high." Bully kept his eyes on the motorcyclists as he pulled his strap from underneath the seat and laid it on his lap. "If they come by here again, I'm a let'em hold this whole mothafucking clip."

Suddenly, the back window of the Chrysler exploded as bullets sprayed though it, chewing up the back of the front seats along with its passengers. Blood splattered everywhere as hot lead spewed through the 300, tattering it and its occupants. The last spent shell-casings from an automatic weapon pinged off of the ground like loose change, smoke rising from their hollow endings.

A disoriented and bloody Bully looked over to Thangz; half her head was missing and her face held the mold of her attempting to scream. Knowing that there wasn't anything that he could do for his lady, Bully swung open the door and the car vomited him into the street. He landed on the surface hard and grimaced, spitting blood and mucus as he struggled to his hands and knees, slicing up his palms on the broken glass that littered the streets.

Vroooooooom!

Bully could hear the squealing of the Kawasaki Ninja as it neared him. Before he knew it the motorcycle came skidding to a halt a foot away from his crimson stained hand. Slowly, he looked up and met the extended barrel of an Uzi .9mm, seeing death present in its hollow ending. He held up his trembling hand and bullets blew it off in chunks when the motorcyclist fired. Bully fell onto his back in agony, clutching his bloody stomp and bawling. The motorcyclist leveled his machinegun and finished him off, leaving a heap of bloody flesh in the middle of the street. The other leather clad rider came running from behind the Chrysler with an Uzi identical to his partner's. This was the nigga that had opened fire on Bully and Thangz from the rear of the car. He hopped onto the back of his partner's Kawasaki Ninja and they sped off down the street.

That night

Stepping out the backdoor of a bar, Supacrip looked down the alley and saw the men he had got into it with inside. One of the men yelled out, "Old hoe ass nigga!" while another shouted, "Why don't chu wolf that shit now?" He didn't pay them any mind, though. He wasn't scared, nor was he intimidated. If the knuckleheads thought he was pussy they were barking up the wrong tree.

Supacrip saw the scowling faces of the men approaching in his peripherals, but he carried on with his business. He removed the joint from behind his ear and slid it between his lips. He reached for the lighter stashed in his small-pocket. While doing so, he brushed his shirt aside and exposed the butt of his pistol. Once the men saw that he was packing, they turned around and headed back to where they came. Supacrip grinned, took a pull from his joint and then blew smoke into the air. He went to take another pull and that's when a pair of hands grabbed him by the face from above. The hands gripped him at the top of his head and under his chin; he struggled before his neck was violently snapped. Supacrip's body slumped and his eyes rolled to their corners. He dropped to his knees and flopped into the alley. A ninja jumped down over him. He looked up and down the alley as he held two fingers to victim's neck, checking his pulse. After confirming his kill, he ran down the alley where he was swallowed by the darkness.

Later that night

The situation with Nightmare had gotten too out of hand. Pavielle's shooters had been dropping bodies all over the city but none of them were his. Nightmare was nowhere to be found. It was like he had vanished into the air. That was okay though, because just as soon as he showed his ugly fucking face, Pavielle was going to make sure that there was someone there to blow it off.

"This is the house?" Gouch asked Pavielle as they both stared out of the front passenger window at an off white house. They had just rolled up in the young kingpin's red 96' Chevy Impala, he executed the engine.

Pavielle glanced at the slip of paper with the address on it, and then back up at the address on the front of the house. "Yeah, this is it." He nodded his head.

"Who are these niggaz out here?" Gouch stared at the Mexican cats loitering in the front yard of the house, while he took casual pulls from a Newport, blowing smoke from his nose.

"The natives," Pavielle looked over into his brother's eyes. "I know you aren't stressing over these niggaz."

"Fuck outta here." Gouch waved him off, looking at him like he was stupid. "You know I keep my Girls with me," he lifted his shirt and exposed the twin Berettas in his waistband. "They dying to give a few busters' mommas something to cry about. You Griff me?" he let his shirt fall back over his bangers. He leaned forth and mashed his cigarette out into the ashtray as he expelled smoke from his nostrils and mouth.

"Come on." Pavielle grabbed the knapsack from off the backseat and opened his door. He stepped out into the cool night's air and made his way around his whip. Together, he and his brother made their way across the street en route to the off white house. The Mexicans that were politicking in the front yard zeroed in on them. The chatter amongst them ceased and they fell into formation at the foot of the steps, creating a human barricade between Pavielle and Gouch, as they entered the front yard. There was one with a shaved head, one with slicked back hair and one who had his hair in a ponytail. They all wore hard faces and either white T-shirts or flannels. The one with the ponytail looked to be in his late 20s, while the others looked to be in their early to mid 30s. He was the shortest and slimmest of the three and the others were muscular in build. Pavielle approached ponytail and placed his hand on his chest, stopping him in his tracks.

"Hold up homie." Ponytail spoke with a stone face and a glint in his eyes. Pavielle peered into the windows of ponytail's soul and saw that a killer lay in them, but he didn't give a fuck. His face twisted and he looked down at ponytail's hand as if it were contagious. Angered, he smacked ponytail's hand down. The assault made a clap sound and right behind it bangers were drawn by everyone except Pavielle. The Mexicans had their weapons pointed in the young kingpin's face, while Gouch had his Girls pointed in theirs.

"Fuck is up with you, homes? You suicidal or something?" ponytail spat with his finger resting on the trigger of his banger.

"Don't chu ever put your fucking hands on me, you're lucky it's still attached to your wrist!" Pavielle popped that shit like he didn't have three guns pointed in his face.

"You've got some set of cojones on you, mayate." The Mexican with the slicked back hair said to him.

"Never mind that," Pavielle waved him off. "I'm here to see Bucho; run along and get your boss, I don't talk to workers."

"You come over here talking shit like God made Adam of Teflon," ponytail said. "I should squeeze this Nina off in your face, pussy!"

Pavielle stared ponytail dead in his eyes and said, "All I'm hearing is a whole lotta talk."

Just as ponytail applied pressure to the trigger, a voice rang out from the darkness. "Krazy, Old Man, Whispers, put your guns down Vatos, that's no way to treat our guests!" Pavielle and Gouch surveyed their surroundings trying to figure out where the voice had come from, but couldn't find it. The Mexicans lowered their bangers and a brother emerged from the shadows of the sun porch, with one hand buried in his pocket while the other fondled with a toothpick in his teeth. He was dressed in a black fedora that he wore pulled low over his brows, a wife-beater and tan Dickies, which he wore high over his navel. His bushy mustache hung well over his top lip. Pavielle observed him attentively as the Mexicans parted and he took his time coming down the steps, one foot at a time until he was dead smack in front of Pavielle.

"What's up, homie? We've been expecting you. I'm Black, but my carnalies call me Negro." He held out his hand. Pavielle looked down at Negro's hand then up into his eyes, extending his own hand. He noticed that although Negro was a brother, he spoke with the accent of a Chicano and had the swagger of a Cholo. Anyone else would have thought that Negro was a black man trying to act like one of the Barrio's own, but the young kingpin could see that he wasn't putting on a show. What you saw was what you got. He was a product of his environment.

Negro turned to Gouch who still had his bangers drawn, raising his hands in surrender. "Chill, homeboy, I come in peace."

"It's bool, Gucci," Pavielle told his big brother. Gouch hesitantly lowered his Girls and tucked them into his waistband.

"Where's Bucho?" Pavielle asked Negro.

"Follow me." Negro motioned for them to follow him inside of the house. Gripping the knapsack tightly, Pavielle fell in line behind him with Gouch bringing up the rear. Gouch made sure he eye-fucked each one of the Mexicans on his way up the steps.

Negro led Pavielle and Gouch inside the house and into the den. Bucho sat watching a Mexican porno, which played out on the big flat-screen TV. The television was so loud that the sound pounced off of the walls and caused them to vibrate. Bucho was a blob of a man that rocked a shaved head with tattoos all over it. He had gold loop earrings in both ears and a bushy goatee. His large frame filled up the black leather sofa he was perched on. His meaty fingers were wrapped around a bottle of Hennessy, which he occasionally took to the head. He wore an icy gold Rolex that was flooded with so many diamonds that you couldn't make out the hands of its clock. On his opposite wrist was a chunky gold, iced out bracelet. Lying over his opened gold and black Versace silk shirt was an icy gold Jesus piece that casted rainbows under the illuminating light of the ceiling fan. Bucho was so engrossed in the skin flick that he hadn't even noticed that he had company. It wasn't until Negro cleared his throat that he casted his eyes in their direction. His large mitt picked up the remote control from his lap and turned off the flat-screen.

"You're Booby, right? I'm Bucho." He extended his hand. Pavielle slapped hands with the blob and introduced Gouch. Gouch threw his head back like *What's up?* And slapped hands with Bucho. "You guys have a seat." Pavielle and Gouch sat down. "Can I get chu anything, something to drink? A blow job, maybe? Yeah? OK. Hey, Negro, hook'em up," Bucho busted up laughing. "Nah, I'm just kidding around guys." He held up his hands in surrender. Gouch kept a stern face while Pavielle gave a halfhearted smirk. Bucho took the bottle to the head and then placed the cork back inside of it. He sat the bottle down on the floor between his legs. He rubbed his hands together and said, "Now, I hear you have a lil' problem on your hands, what's his name?" he wore a serious face as he threw his hefty arm over the top of the sofa. Pavielle pulled Nightmare's mug shot from inside of his jacket and passed it to him.

Pavielle spoke as Bucho examined the picture, David Grant A.k.a Nightmare. This mothafucka has been a thorn in side. He's killed more of my homies than I can count on one hand, he's put my family in danger and on top of that he's fucking my money up. A nigga can't eat like he used to with this lil' beef we got going. I want this clown dead, and I've been told that you're just the man I need to holla at to get the job done."

Bucho nodded in agreement. "You've tried the rest, now try the best." He laid Nightmare's mug shot down on the arm of the sofa. "I'll put my best squad on it. In the next few days this will have all seemed like a bad dream. Did you bring the fedia, homie?"

Pavielle nodded and tossed Bucho the knapsack. He in turn tossed it over to Negro. "That's forty bands; you'll get the other forty bands once the jobs done, just like we discussed." The blob nodded and then nodded to Negro who grabbed a money-counting machine and sat down to run the money through it. Pavielle and Bucho shot the shit while Negro ran the money through the machine. Once he was done he looked to his boss and gave him a thumb up.

"Alright, the fedia checks out, I'll give you the confirmation once the job is done." Bucho told him. He slapped hands with Pavielle and Gouch before they left.

Chapter 9

Pavielle sat on the couch punishing a bottle of champagne in the comfort of his newly built home. When he had the place built he had it installed with arguably the best home security system in the world. He put surveillance cameras on the inside and outside of the place so he could see who was coming and going. He also put bars on every window and bought two more Rottweilers just as vicious as Damu. The young kingpin made his lavish home harder to get into than Fort Knox.

Pavielle poured a little champagne out onto the mink carpet for the homies he lost in the war. He then said a prayer for his loved ones and crossed his himself in the sign of the crucifix.

"Booby, it's Gouch and Killa, open up!" Gouch's voice came from over the intercom.

Pavielle picked up the surveillance monitor/control panel from the couch and pressed a button on it that unlocked the gate to his home. Moments later, there was a knock on the door. He looked through the peephole before unlocking the door and pulling it open. He stood to the side as Gouch and

Killa Dre filed inside over the threshold. He then closed the door shut behind them and flopped down on the couch.

"So, what's up y'all? I know this ain't a social call." Pavielle took the champagne to the head, guzzling it. His throat moved up and down his neck as he drunk thirstily from the bottle.

"Damn, nigga, be easy." Gouch frowned seeing his brother drink recklessly from the champagne bottle. "Anyway, your man and his girl are no longer with us."

"And Supacrab? You never told me what was up with him." Pavielle asked.

"I shouldn't have to, my nigga. You know better than the homies how big bruh gets down." Gouch reminded him of all of the work that he saw him put in it. He then grabbed a banana from the fruit bowl and peeling it.

"Is it bool, O.G?" Killa Dre pointed to an apple on the fruit table, wondering if he could have it.

"Help yourself." Pavielle told him and then turned to Gouch. "Any word on our boy?"

"Nah," Gouch shook his head and took a bite of the banana. "That fool lying low somewhere and calling shots from a far, but don't worry we're gone run a gas line through his rabbit-hole and when his black ass comes running out, old

Killa's gonna bash him in the head. Ain't that right, Y.G?" Killa Dre nodded in agreement and took a bite of his apple.

"If something's going to happen to this nigga then it needs to happen now," Pavielle said seriously, frustration plastered on his face. "Ortiz and Arsenegger are up my ass, and bodies are piling to the height of the Empire State building. If things keep going like this I'm going to be dead or in jail."

"Blood, you're tripping," Gouch sat down on the arm of the couch. "You got forty thousand dollars in the streets. Do you know what a nigga will do for forty thousand dollars? All of these young goon ass niggaz running around bodying mothafuckaz for nothing, now they've gotta reason. I'm telling you, Blood, in the next few days one of these young hardheads gone come walking up with old boy's head in a grocery bag. Watch and see." He took another bite of his banana.

"Yeah, you're probably right." Pavielle told him before guzzling more of the champagne.

"Oh, you didn't see Killa's face, huh?" Gouch finished off the banana and tossed the peel aside on the table.

"Unh uh," Pavielle shook his head.

"Come here, Y.G." Gouch snapped his fingers and mo-tioned Killa Dre over. The youth ascended on Pavielle taking bites out of his apple. Pavielle sat up on the couch to get a good look at his little homie's face.

Killa Dre had tear drops tattooed on the corner of his right-eye. OLS was inked over his right lid and RTBG was inked over his left. Pavielle could tell the inks were new because they had A & D Ointment on them. "What chu think, big homie?" he smiled, stretching his thick blackened lips across his face. He'd been a smoker for quite some time so the change to them was permanent. "Gouch blasted me a couple hours ago." Pavielle thought that the tattoos made Killa Dre look menacing. The tattoos coupled with his gangster attire made him look like what he was: a coldblooded killer down for his set.

Pavielle realized that his little homie's innocents had been stripped from him. The young boy was banging, slanging, and gun ranging and Pavielle was partially responsible for this. It would be one of the many things he'd be paying for when he walked through the rusted, burning gates of hell.

"Gangsta," Pavielle replied, giving Killa Dre a pound. "I was thinking about getting mine done but you beat me to it, my nigga."

"Told you your big bro ain't nothing to fuck with on that ink-gun." Gouch bragged, rubbing his hands together.

"Yeah, I might have you put the hood on my back with an illustration of a grimy ass city, or something." Pavielle told him.

"That would be hard as a mothafucka." Gouch gave him a pound.

Two days later

Nightmare ran down Crenshaw Boulevard like he had a lynch mob on his heels. Automatic gunfire trailed behind him shattering the glass windows of businesses and spilling broken glass out onto the sidewalk. He fired blindly over his shoulder at the Navigator of Mexican assassins on his tail. He was nearing the center of the block when a burly brother emerged from the weed shop playing with a dragon head Zippo lighter, flicking the flame on and off. Nightmare dove to the sidewalk and a wave of bullets came right behind him, tatting up the burly nigga'z chest. He hit the sidewalk hard, Zippo lighter skidding across the ground.

Nightmare tried to run into the weed shop, but the owner slammed the door in him.

"Shit!" his head snapped from left to right, feeling like a cornered rat with nowhere to go with the killers zeroing in on him. Seeing how large the fella was that had gotten stretched the fuck out, a light bulb came on inside of his head. That's when he drew his other Desert Eagle and ran forth.

The Navigator truck carrying the Mexican assassins halted at the center of the block. The driver stayed behind the wheel along with the front seat passenger while the other two assassins hopped out from the backseat, one by one. One was wearing a gray hoodie and the other was wearing a jean jacket and shades. They both wore blue bandanas over the lower halves of their faces. Weapons in hand, they slowly moved in on Nightmare firing their Ingrams, turning the human form he was stashed behind into a heap of bloody hamburger. The Mexican assassins laughed devilishly as they swept their weapons back and forth across the mutilated corpse. The shell-casings flying from their Ingrams sounded like coins as they hit the pavement.

"Stop playing with that fool, homes! Finish that punk! I'm tryna collect tonight." The driver yelled from behind the wheel, clutching a banger of his own. He had on a pair of shades that he wore backwards on his head.

The two Mexican assassins ejected their spent magazines from their Ingrams, letting them deflect off of the surface. When Nightmare heard their empty magazines hit the street, he knew they were reloading and he had to react fast. Resting the butts of his Desert Eagles on the gut of the corpse, he steadied his handguns and opened fire on the assassin in the gray hoodie. Hollow-tip rounds cracked off, striking their mark in the kneecap, thigh, and gut.

"Arghhhh," Gray hoodie's face twisted into a mask of pain before he collapsed into the street. The assassin in the jean jacket and shades had just smacked a fresh magazine into his Ingram. As soon as he went to point it, some hot shit blew his ass off of his feet, sending his shades up in the air.

"Pinche puto cabrone!" the driver scowled, swinging open his door, ready to put a body on his gun. The passenger, who was cradling a shotgun, had grabbed the handle of his door and was moving to hop out when twin blinding lights shined in through the windshield. He held a hand over his brows trying to see what was headed for him. By the time he realized it was another vehicle it was too late. Nightmare's Cadillac collided with the Navigator head on, sending scrap metal and wreckage spilling into the street.

A dazed Bobby Blue slowly exited the Cadillac; there was a nasty gash above her brow. She regained her composure and looked around; everyone had expired except the front seat passenger and the driver. He lay as a bloody mess on the boulevard, but his fingers still twitched with a flicker of life. Bobby Blue's face contracted with animosity and she grabbed her gun from underneath the driver seat of the Caddy. She stalked over to the passenger side window of the Navigator and pressed her banger into rider's skull, spraying his brains on the driver. The drivers face was plastered with blood and bits of brain; he narrowed his eyes into slits and screamed for God's mercy, so she sent him to his kingdom.

"Come on! We've gotta get outta here!" Nightmare grabbed Bobby's hand and they hauled ass down the boulevard, feet hurriedly making tracks as they occasionally looked over their shoulders for the police. People spilled out onto the sidewalk from nearby businesses to see what all the commotion was. Once Nightmare and Bobby put enough distance between them and the murder scene, they slowed to a trot and concealed their bangers. They hopped on the Metro bus, paid their fair, and moved all the way to the back. Bobby rested her head against Nightmare's shoulder and shut her eyelids. Nightmare leaned his head back and took a breather, thankful to have escaped with his life.

Nightmare was for sure that he had a bounty on his head now. This was the second time a band of Mexican assassins had gotten at him. With hit squads coming at him this hard he knew that it was only a matter of time before his head was mounted over Pavielle's fireplace. Shit had just gotten real, and it was time for him to turn it up.

Chapter 10

Pavielle sat out three red dog bowls of Kibbles & Bits mixed with steak in the backyard. The bowls were labeled Damu, Devil, and Badass. He then whistled for his dogs, all of whom were playing on the lawn, "Damu, Devil, and Demon! Y'all niggaz come eat!" he motioned the four legged beasts over and they came running, tongues hanging out of their mouths as they panted.

"That gunpowder you mixed with their food gone make them meaner than a bitch," Gouch declared taking pulls from a blunt and blowing smoke into air.

"They're already meaner than a mothafucka," Pavielle assured him, rubbing Devil behind his ears as he ate out of his bowl. "This shit gone make'em brazy, though. That's how I want 'em 'cause as soon as a fool call himself hopping my fence, they gone chew his ass into burger." Gouch passed him the blunt and he took a few pulls, releasing the smoke through his nostrils. The oldest Hood brother pulled a bottle of Cognac from a brown paper bag, sat out two plastic cups, and poured them up. Pavielle's cell rang and he answered it, placing it to his ear. "Who this?" he spoke into his cellular. "Meeting about what? Hello? Hello?"

"Who that?" Gouch asked.

"Black Jesus, he wants to see me."

Gouch shrugged his shoulders, "For what?"

"I don't know, but he wants to see me now. He sounded serious, too."

"Well, I'm going with you. I done seen way too many movies where they send for a nigga and whack'em as soon as he gets there."

Pavielle shrugged his shoulders and said, "Let's roll."

An hour later

The young kingpin rolled up to the golden gates that lead to the path of Black Jesus' estate. Before he could press the button on the intercom he was buzzed in. He looked to Gouch and he pointed to the surveillance cameras on the corners of the gates, letting him know that they were being watched. With that in mind, he drove up the driveway and murdered the engine. No sooner than the headlights died and the engine went out, there was a knock on his window. It startled him and Gouch. When they turned around they found themselves face to face with a shiny, chrome revolver. Julio greeted him with a shit eating grin and a wave of his hand. Gouch went for his strap and heard a light tap on his window, whipping his head around he discovered Tango and his .45.

"Get the fuck outta the car! Now!" he demanded, snatching open the door and yanking Gouch's ass out of that mothafucka.

Gouch and Pavielle were made to get in the back of Black Jesus' stretch white Mercedes Benz. Inside they found Black Jesus cradling a Tommy-gun. He was sitting across from his little brother, Bullet, who was playing Super Street Fighter 5 on an Ipad. A lit blunt dangled from the corner of his mouth. Julio climbed in followed by Tango, who closed the door behind them. The stretch Mercedes resurrected and made to leave the golden gates of the mansion.

"Yo, Jesus, what's the deal, fam?" Pavielle asked worried.

"You check them for weapons?" Black Jesus asked Tango, ignoring the young kingpin.

"Yeah," Tango answered handing over the brothers' weapons. Black Jesus took the straps and stashed them into a secret compartment.

"That's on my momma, Blood, if you touch my brother I'm a..." that was as far as Gouch got before Tango busted him in the head with the butt of his gun, bloodying the lower half of his face. Pavielle tried to rush Tango, but Julio hit him in the stomach with his revolver, knocking the wind out of him. Angry, he glared up at him holding himself.

"Don't be stupid, homeboy." Julio whispered to Pavielle with his pistol pressed into his gut, wishing that he would test his G so he could put a hole in his ass.

What the fuck have I gotten myself into? Pavielle thought as he shook his head.

An hour and a half later

The stretch Benz pulled deep into the woods. Julio and Tango climbed out with Gouch and Pavielle at gun point. They were followed by Black Jesus and Bullet who traded in his Ipad for a .380. Flashlights in hand, they made their way through the woods with the others in tow, twigs snapping beneath their shoes.

"I'm not going out like a sucker, Booby." Gouch whispered to Pavielle, slightly turning his head toward him. As soon as the words left his mouth he was shoved from the back by Tango.

"Shut the fuck up and keep walking!" Tango barked.

"You're pretty tough with that strap in your hand, old man. I'd like to see what chu can do without it." Gouch spoke with a mad dog face, walking beside Pavielle.

"Plenty," Tango responded. "Golden Gloves, asshole, '73, now keep walking." He shoved him forward causing him to stumble forward a little.

"Here we are," Black Jesus announced coming upon two six foot graves, shining his flashlight over them both. He motioned for Tango and Julio to bring Pavielle and Gouch over.

Stepping forth, Pavielle and Gouch looked over the two graves and knew what was to happen next.

"I wanna know what the fuck is this shit about!" Pavielle asked the drug lord. "If you gone kill me, I wanna at least know what the fuck I'm dying for."

"Don't play stupid, you know exactly what this is about." Black Jesus responded.

"Blood, if I knew I wouldn't be asking your mothafucking ass, now would…" that was as far as Pavielle got before Julio smacked him across the head with his revolver. He winced in pain, touching the back of his skull. His fingers came away with blood.

"You wanna know what this is about? Alright, I'll tell you," Black Jesus nodded his head. "This whole thing is about three things: loyalty, respect and honor, and the men who live by those three words. The few who do are in the minority and are what we street cats like to call, stand up guys. Following the rules and codes separates us street guys from the fall down guys. Isn't that right, Tango?"

"Arghh," Tango howled in agony, clutching his wounded hand which had a hole in it. Julio had turned his revolver from Pavielle's head and shot him. He then kicked the gun that the Dominican bodyguard dropped into one of the graves. "You treacherous dog," He spat in Julio's direction. Pavielle and Gouch exchanged glances. They didn't know what the fuck was going on.

"Treacherous?" Black Jesus raised an eyebrow. He couldn't believe this mothafucka had the nerve to call someone Treacherous. "Look who's fucking talking!" he blasted Tango in the stomach with his Tommy-gun. He doubled over holding himself and gritting his teeth, trying to fight back the ball of fire growing inside of his stomach.

"Ah, you son of a bitch," Tango cursed him. The pain was wreaking havoc on his insides.

"You see this piece of shit right here?" Black Jesus pointed his Tommy at Tango, but asked Pavielle the question. "He and my father were best friends coming up. The two of them and my father's brother had their own little crew they use to run with back in the day. They were family. They knew each other since they were seven years old. We've known this bastard all our lives. When my poppa died he became like a father to me and my little brother." Tears ran down Black Jesus' face as he talked, dripping off of his chin. "You'd think that would have stopped him from hitting my shipment of cocaine when it dropped, or orchestrating a plan to have me and my people belly up. Why would someone who's supposed to be like family to me do such a thing? I'll tell you why, so he could be the man; the head spic in charge." He mad dogged Tango. The drug lord was so hot that it appeared that steam was rising from his head.

"Jesus, it wasn't me, papi. I swear on my mother's soul." He lied as he crossed himself in the sign of the crucifix. "It was all Julio. You've gotta believe me! I swear to God!" He said with his hands together in prayer, his pleading eyes staring up at the man whose mercy he wanted.

"Oh, don't start bitching up now!" Julio told him, looking down at him with his gun clutched at his side. "You wanted to be head spic in charge, remember?"

"Sell out ass mothafucka." Bullet finally spoke, shaking his head. He was looking at Tango in disgust.

"You're probably wondering where your godson and his friends are. Well, don't worry; I had someone take good care of them." Black Jesus informed him, caressing his Tommy-gun affectionately.

Earlier that night

Money Making Nate came out of his house on his cell phone flanked by his cousin Man Man and Barry. "Aye, amigo, I'm on my way." Nate said into his cell before hanging up and hopping into his whip. He resurrected the engine and that's when he saw a 4'11 dark figure roll from underneath the car and take off running. "What the fuck?" he frowned, grabbing his pistol with one hand and the door handle with the other.

"What's up, cousin?" Man Man asked. Nate opened the door, and as soon as his foot touched the street his car exploded, scattering burning wreckage everywhere.

Present

"You mothafucka," Tango stuggled up to his feet cradling his wounded hand, he yelled as he took off in Black Jesus' direction. Seeming as if he didn't have a care in the world, the drug lord produced a cigar from his suit and took his time lighting it up. Tango got within three feet of him before Julio shot him in the back of the head, sending him falling awkwardly into one of the graves. The lazy eyed Vato crossed his himself in the sign of the crucifix as he stared down into the grave at Tango.

Blam!

Julio's eyes bulged and his head snapped to the left. Smoke wafted from the back of his dome as he dropped down to his knees and dropped his revolver. He fell face first into the grave as Bullet lowered his smoking .380. The youngest Arturo brother harped up some phlegm and spat it into Julio's grave; it splattered on impact when it hit his face.

"I cannot, and will not, allow an individual without any principals, or moral values to work for me. If it weren't for Julio pulling my coattail to what Tango had planned for me I would have chalked it up as a lost. He auctioned his man's life away for a spot on my team and one million dollars in cash. With friends like these, I ask you, 'Who needs enemies?'" He looked from Pavielle to Gouch. They didn't say a word because they were fucked up about how shit had just unfolded.

"What the hell happened here?"

"Tango wanted me to believe that you and your people were the ones that hit my shipment, but I found out otherwise."

Pavielle took a deep breath and bowed his head, massaging the bridge of his nose. His nerves were all fucked up after what had almost went down. Gouch stepped beside him and gripped his shoulder affectionately.

Seeing how affected Pavielle was about what happened, the drug lord went on to speak.

"My apologies for using you as bait," he began. "I trust you both will find a way for me to make it up to you."

"Oh, I'ma think of something." Pavielle assured him as he grabbed a shovel. "Come on, Gucci. Let's bury these fools so we can get the fuck up from outta here."

Gouch grabbed a shovel and he and his brother went about the business of throwing dirt into the graves onto the dead bodies.

Chapter 11

Nightmare purchased a chocolate brown '78 El Camino from a private owner off the corner of Central and Century. He and Bobby Blue took refuge at the mother of all shitty motels. The motel was acquired because he believed no one would look for him in such a dump. He had a reputation for being a hood nigga with expensive taste. He'd be expected to stay in five star hotels like the one he had previously stayed in, not some hole in the wall in the ghetto.

Nightmare shaved off his goatee and had Bobby Blue put eight cornrows in his head. He looked himself over in the mirror. With the recent weight gain he looked like a totally different person. He believed that even his own mother wouldn't be able to recognize him.

While Bobby Blue took a shower, Nightmare put in a phone call to his capo, Taco.

"What's cripilating, big homie?" Taco answered on the third ring.

"Just planted ten toes down," Nightmare responded. "So this slob nigga Booby done marked The Loc for death, huh? A nigga gotta shake the city, but before I go, I'ma pimp slap his bitch ass."

"What chu got in mind?"

"The Ghost."

"Shit, Cuz, why didn't you sic The Ghost on this nigga before?"

"Nigga is expensive, but I'ma get the job done. So, look, I'm a need you to collect my scratch from the traps for me. I'ma have Bobby come pick it up later on tonight."

"Alright."

"Alright, Cuz, stay up."

"All day," Taco replied before hanging up.

Bobby Blue came out of the bathroom wrapped in a towel and combing her hair to the back. She sat on the bed beside her mom. "So, did you talk to Taco yet?"

"Yeah, he's putting together that paper now. I told him I was going to send you by there to get it tonight."

"I feel sorry for that boy if you're really getting The Ghost on him," Bobby shook her head. Her face and shoulders were glistening from her showering. "You know my friend Danielle that works at the beauty salon over on Crenshaw? Well, she told me her uncle's homeboy was fooling around with this Italian guy's wife who's connected to the mafia and he put The Ghost on them. She said The Ghost slashed the throat of the guy that had been having an affair with his wife and pulled his tongue out through the hole in his neck. Right after, he sliced off the wife's clit so that she couldn't feel any..."

The rest of the sentence died in her throat when Nightmare pulled a blue velvet box from his pocket. He smiled from ear to ear when he said to her, "You've been working pretty hard out there, how about a promotion?"

Bobby Blue turned around and met the twinkling of a platinum, diamond engagement ring. Tears danced at the corners of her eyes and she smiled, revealing two rows of pearly white teeth.

"Oh, daddy, it's beautiful." She put her hands over her mouth, tears jetting down her cheeks. Nightmare took her hand and slid the engagement ring onto her finger. "Daddy, I love it. Yes, I'll marry you." She took him by the face and kissed him all over it. "What happens now?"

"What happens now is you love me, be loyal, and hold me down like you've been doing. Can you do that?" she nodded yes and kissed him all over his face again, hugging him lovingly. "I need you to pick up that money. I need it if I'm going to pay this man to get rid of this nigga Booby for me. The longer he's alive, the longer we'll have to postpone our wedding."

"I better get on it then." She gave him a quick peck on the lips and hopped out of bed to get dressed.

***

Bobby Blue knocked on the door of Taco's house. As she waited for someone to answer, she took a cautious look over her shoulder to make sure no one had followed her; the coast was clear. A moment later, Taco opened the door and gave her the once over. Behind the Channel shades, the blondee wig and the hoodie, he barely recognized her. He figured her duds were to throw off any fools looking to snatch her and use her to bait Nightmare so they could kill him for the bounty money.

"What's up, Ms. Blue?" Taco greeted her.

"How you doing?" she asked. "You got that for me?"

"Here," he handed her a duffle bag full of money. She took a quick glance inside and slung it over her shoulder. "Where did you park? I'ma walk you to your car." He told her, stashing his banger in his waistband and laying his shirt over it.

Bobby smiled. "It's nice to see shivery isn't dead."

"Come on, girl." He smiled as he made for the steps.

***

Vayda pulled to a stop light singing Love by Keisha Cole at the top of her lungs. She was performing like she was in front of a sold out crowd at Madison Square Garden. Little momma bobbed her head to the beat, pounding the steering wheel with her fist rhythmically. She could feel someone watching her so she looked to the El Camino beside her. The driver whipped her head back around and slumped down into the seat.

"Hmmph," Vayda starting the song over as she drove through the green light.

***

"Baby, I got the money from Taco, I'm finna be on my way back. You want anything to eat? Alright, well, I'll be there in a minute." Bobby pressed end and tossed her cell into the passenger seat. A violet Benz Kompressor pulled to a stop beside her. She looked over to the driver and her jaw dropped. "Vayda?" the woman in the Kompressor looked over to Bobby and she turned her head and slumped down in the seat. Once the light turned green Vayda drove off and she pulled off to follow her. Immediately, she thought back to the photo Nightmare had shown her of Pavielle and his girl. He told her their names and what they were to each other. Homegirl in the Benz was the exact same bitch she saw in the photo.

"Yeahhhh, I'ma follow this bitch." Bobby told herself and kept a safe distance from her as she trailed behind her, being incognito.

***

Vayda pulled into the driveway of her and Pavielle's new home. She hopped out with two shopping bags and a box of food from Outback Steak House. Little did she know, parked four houses down and across the street was Bobby Blue, watching her like a stalker.

Bobby smiled sinisterly seeing Vayda closing the door behind her as she stepped inside of the house. She hoped that Pavielle was home waiting for his lady's return, so she could kill two birds with one stone. Nightmare would be very proud of her once he found out that she was responsible for murking the trap god and his bitch. If there was one thing that Bobby loved to do it was please her man.

Bobby hopped out the car and jogged across the street, occasionally looking over her shoulder to make sure no one was watching her. Leaning against the fence of Pavielle's estate, she peeked into his front yard and saw his guard dogs lying around. She pulled herself upon the barbwire fence and walked it like a tightrope, careful not to get tangled up in the barbwire. Her foot hit an empty Coca Cola bottle and it rocked back and forth, threatening to topple. Bobby gasped, hoping the bottle wouldn't fall. Her heart dropped when she saw the bottle hit the ground, alerting the three beasts to her presence. She jumped down and scooped the bottle up, taking a hold of it. Next, she produced her gun and stuck it into the bottle, using it as a muzzle. The dogs snarled and snapped at her, Damu leapt forward and she pulled the trigger of her weapon.

Meanwhile

Vayda relieved her bladder upon the commode. You'd think she was being orally pleasured from the expression on her face. She heard the dogs barking and hurried to her feet, wiping her pussy. By the time she pulled her pants up the barking stopped. She took a peek out of the bathroom window and didn't see the dogs. Suddenly, the lights inside the house went out and she began to panic, heart pounding inside of her chest. Vayda was scared but she tried to keep herself at ease. Cautiously, she felt around in the dark until she found the light-switch. Next, she flipped the switch off and on, but there was no light. She leaned against the corridor wall and traveled along it until she met the kitchen's entrance, slithering inside like a cat burglar. Hastily, she rummaged through all the kitchen drawers until she found what she was looking for: a box of matches.

Vayda wandered into the living room where she kept her Vanilla scented candles on the glass top table. Using the light shining in through the barred windows from the outside, she was able to locate it. When she went to pick up the candle, something came crashing through the moon-roof in the ceiling, startling her. She looked down and saw Damu lying at her feet, bleeding. Vayda screamed in a panic and grabbed the candle from off the table. She tried to strike a flame with a match, but couldn't manage. She was so terrified her hands were trembling and she ended up dropping the box of matches. The matches came spilling out of the box onto the floor, scattering everywhere. She got down on her knees and picked up a match. Next, she picked herself up from the floor and struck the match. A flame hissed to life and she lit the candle. She turned around and met the murderous, blood thirsty eyes of a woman she'd never laid eyes on before. The color in her face drained and gave her a paler complexion. She could have pissed on herself when she saw Bobby. The Amazon blew out the flame of the candle and punched her square in the face, breaking her nose. Blood came spilling from her nose as she crashed to the floor, dropping the candle. With the lower half of her face masked with blood, she crawled towards the kitchen with Bobby taunting her all the way.

"I bet chu wondering what this ass whipping is for, huh? Well, since your man has come on the scene, my nigga'z pockets have become a lil' light and we not feeling that!" She kicked Vayda hard as shit in her side, cracking her ribs. Vayda's eyes snapped open as she howled from the explosion of pain she experienced. Slipping on a pair of black leather gloves, Bobby cracked her knuckles and went to work on the redbone. She punched, kicked, and stomped her, not giving a mad ass fuck about her being pregnant. The Amazon grabbed a fist full of her victim's curly hair and yanked her head back violently, causing her to holler out. Her eyes were bugged and she was gasping for air, face shiny from perspiration. Pulling homegirl to her feet, Bobby walked her inside of the kitchen where she proceeded to slam her face into the counter repeatedly, leaving smears of blood behind. Vayda's eyes rolled to the back of her skull and she looked like she was about to faint.

"Don't go dying on me now!" Bobby scowled and gritted, still holding her up by her hair. "I'm not done with cho light bright ass yet, hoe!" she dog-walked her ass over to the glass table, hoisted her above her head, and slammed her on it. The table exploded into pieces, scattering broken glass everywhere.

Vayda hit the surface wincing. Fearing for her unborn child's life, she balled up into a fetal position. Bobby withdrew her banger from her waistband and pointed it at Vayda's face, finger curling around the trigger. Just as she was giving the trigger pressure a sharp pain shot up her foot and she clenched her jaws to thwart it off. Looking down, she saw that Vayda had driven a jagged piece of glass into her foot, leaving it sticking straight up. Bobby clocked her upside of the head with the butt of her weapon and she hit the floor on her side, breathing hard. Gritting her teeth, Bobby kneeled down to pull the glass out of her foot. As soon as she wrapped her hand around the glass, Vayda shot up to her feet with another piece of jagged glass. Growling, she drove the glass into the side of her assailant's neck and blood pissed out of the side of it.

"Ahhhhhhh," Bobby's eyelids snapped open and she hollered at the top of her lungs. She dropped her gun and grabbed her wound with both hands, trying to stop the blood from squirting out of it. A look of agony and confusion crossed her eyes. She looked at Vayda accusingly before falling flat on her face, legs flailing in the air.

Boom!

Pavielle kicked open the door and sent splinters flying. He charged through the door holding his banger at his side with both hands.

"Holy shit," He said, taking in the bloody mess that was Vayda. He went to rush to her aid, but stalled once he saw Bobby reaching for her gun, which lay amid the broken glass.

Bloc!

Bloc!

Three copper bullets spat from Pavielle's .9mm causing it to jump. The two shots struck her in the chest, laying her flat on her stomach. She lay there bleeding and breathing weakly.

Pavielle rushed over to Vayda wrapping her tight in his arms. She sobbed as he rubbed her back soothingly, rocking her back and forth. "It's okay. I'm here now. Everything's going to be alright." He assured her, pulling out his cellular and pressing buttons rapidly, calling 9-1-1.

Three hours later

"Damn, Blood, that's fucked up what happened to Booby's girl." Killa Dre told Gouch as he cracked open a swisher.

"You know what time it is, right?" Gouch said from the couch where he watched Mike Tyson's greatest knockouts.

"Oh, you know how I do." Killa Dre said, dumping the swisher's guts into the trash can.

"You sound like you get a kick outta doing dirt, my nigga."

"Niggaz smoked my brother, I'm a make their hood feel it everytime I get a chance, feel me?"

"Frankenstein's monster."

"What?"

"Me and baby bro created a monster with chu, kid."

Killa Dre laughed. "What're you talking about?"

"Nigga, you went from Leave it to Beaver to O-Dog from Menace."

"Hey, it's either in you or it's not." he licked the swisher closed.

"Right," Gouch retorted. "I don't know when baby bro want us to make this move, but chu have that murder gear ready."

"Yezzir," Killa responded lighting the swisher closed.

Chapter 12

Pavielle sat beside Vayda's bed with her fingers inter-locked between his. Vayda suffered a concussion, two broken ribs and a fractured skull.

"You mean that girl that broke into the house is Night-mare's woman?" Vayda questioned from the bed with lines running across her forehead. Her face was swollen and her head was bandaged up, as well as her ribs. Bobby Blue had put hands on that ass.

"Yeah," Pavielle nodded as he caressed his fiancée's hand lovingly, "She's still alive, too. They've got her down the hall."

"With all of those holes you put in her?" she lifted her eyebrows surprised. "The Lord must really be watching over her ass."

"That's what I said." Pavielle wore an expression that let her know that he was just as surprised as she was. As soon as he had popped Bobby's ass up, he called 9-1-1 and then he hit his attorney on his jack and told him to get his ass down at the precinct ASAP. When he made it down to the station he hollered at the interviewing detective whom coincidently happened to be one of his clients. As a favor he forged the paperwork and agreed to replace the gun in the shooting with a registered one later. A couple of hours later Pavielle was a free man. He put the attorney's fees on his tab and had him take him to get his car so that he could go see his boo. Now here he was, right by her side, like he wanted to be. "I don't see how that bitch got in there, fucking alarm system." He shook his head disappointedly, thinking it was a goddamn shame how the expensive system had failed him and put his family in danger. "Piece of shit, I'm sorry, baby," He hung his head, pitying himself.

"Aye, aye," Vayda lifted his chin up with a curled finger, looking into his eyes. "Don't beat yourself up about it. Me and the baby are still here and we're fine, okay?"

"Unh, huh," He nodded his head, tears dancing at the corners of his eyes. The thought of losing her and the baby had scared the shit out of him. He rose from the chair and leaned into her, kissing her romantically while holding the side of her face. Next, he slid down to her protruding belly and pressed his head against it. Feeling a slight kick, his eyes widen with excitement and he smiled, caressing her mound. "Baby, he kicked, did you feel that?" he looked up at her smiling face and she nodded. He then kissed her stomach and stood erect.

"Babe, I'ma go use the bathroom, I'll be back, okay?" she nodded and he leaned forward, bringing her hand to his lips and kissing it like a gentlemen being introduced to a lady.

"Okay." She frowned, looking over his shoulder and seeing a couple African American men standing outside the door. They were all in suits and wore either bowties or ties. These niggaz were strapped, too. The slight bulges in their suits made that apparent. The brothers were trained for armed and unarmed combat and would lay down their lives in the line of duty if necessary, "Baby, who are those men?"

"My relative, Lenny Jihad, sent them over to watch over you. They're some of Farrakhan's personal bodyguards. Them cats right there don't play."

"Oh, okay."

"I'll be right back, babe." He kissed her again before taking his leave.

***

After being harassed by the cop who was assigned to watch Bobby, Nightmare was free to enter her room. He found her handcuffed to the bed, hooked up to a variety of machines. There were tubes running in and out of her body and an incubation tube was down her throat. She was so high off morphine she could barely tell that it was him that entered her room.

With an out stretched hand, Bobby motioned for her man to come to her side. He pulled a chair up to her bedside and took her hand, caressing it gently while staring into her eyes. Although he was on the verge of tears, he couldn't allow them to fall. He didn't know how he knew it, but this would be his lover's final hour.

"Hey, Bobby, can you hear me?" he mustered up a half ass smile to console her. She nodded weakly. "Tell me who did this to you, and on the gang I'm a have niggaz dying and mommas crying." He swore with the utmost sincerity.

Bobby tried to say something, but the incubation tube stopped her from forming the words. Seeing this, Nightmare rummaged through the dresser drawer until he produced an ink pen and a piece of paper. He placed the pen into her freehand and sat the napkin down, watching as she jotted something down. Once she was done he picked up the napkin and read over it, his lips whispering what his mind was being fed.

"Pavielle and Vayda did this to you?" Nightmare frowned and squared his jaws, showcasing the bone structure in them. "He's dead. They both are. I promise you that." He squeezed his fist so tight that the veins in his hand bulged. "You recover my trap?"

Bobby nodded yes and scribbled down the address to the whereabouts of the car. Nightmare picked up the napkin and shoved it into his pocket, rising to his feet, he said, "I'll be back tomorrow. I'll have to see about getting you an attorney and baking a cake for this slob and this fool ass bitch." He swept the loose strands of hair from out of her beautiful face and kissed her tenderly on the forehead. Next, he turned to leave, but she held fast to his hand. His forehead indented and he looked to her, wondering what was on her mind. She tried to say something, but the incubation tube made it difficult. All she ended up doing was coughing and gagging.

"Shhhhhhh!" he hushed her while patting her hand affectionately. "I know, and I love you, too." He kissed her hand before making his departure.

Making his way down the hospital corridor, Nightmare saw a foursome of African American men loitering outside a patient's door. He could tell by their attire that they were Muslims; members of the Nation of Islam, no doubt. He gave them the once over from behind his shades and they gave him a nod. The nigga ignored their acknowledgements and strolled on, passing the men's restroom. As he cleared the restroom's doorway, Pavielle came out wiping his damp hands on his shirt as he headed back to Vayda's room. Had they crossed paths all hell would have broke loose, but luckily they didn't.

The Lord works in mysterious ways.

***

Bobby smiled and shut her eyes, replaying Nightmare's words in her head: I love you, too. She'd heard him say it before, but nothing made her feel more at ease then hearing them once again before she left this world for the next. Tears outlined her eyelashes before they came flooding down her cheeks. There were three last beeps from the heart monitor before its squiggly line went flat and sounded a dreadful siren that signified her departure from this life to the next.

Beeeeeeeep!

Bobby's lips peeled apart and she released her last breath into the world, "Haaaaaa!"

Chapter 13

Three days later

Quite a bit of people turned out for Bobby Blue's funeral. Most people came to see if Nightmare would show up; he didn't, but if he had he would have surely been killed. The bounty on his head had been doubled, so he knew fools would be looking to blow his brains out. Nightmare was nobody's fool though. He came to the funeral, but he played the background wearing a disguise. His get-up was so good that no one recognized him, not even Taco.

The funeral that Nightmare put together for Bobby Blue was one worthy of Princess Diane. Her coffin was white marble with gold handles. She wore a solid gold Tiara decorated with her birthstone and a white dress that would have made Cinderella leave the ball and go home to change clothes. Her hands held a dozen of the most beautiful roses at her waist.

Bobby's body was loaded into a white on white horse & carriage and road throughout the hood she was born in before being delivered to Compton Cemetery. Before her coffin was lowered into the earth a flock of doves were set free and fireworks were popped.

All of the funeral attendees cleared out of the cemetery after the ceremony, except Taco. He was staying behind to make sure Bobby was put into the ground, like Nightmare had instructed him to. Taco watched as dirt was shoveled into the six foot plot Bobby Blue's coffin was placed in. Feeling someone creeping up behind him, he spent around on his heels and drew his banger. He was about to dump on the burly man in the trench coat behind him until he spoke.

"Chill, it's me, Loc!" the burly man said in a hushed tone and then looked around cautiously to make sure no one was watching him.

"Who the fuck is me, Cuz?" Taco's nose was scrunched up and he had his burner pointed right at his ass.

"Nightmare," the burly man removed his shades to show it was him behind the disguise. Taco sighed with relief and tucked his gun. "Cuz, with that gut and fake beard you kind of look like a black Santa Claus and shit." The youngster cracked a smile. Not in the mood for jokes, Nightmare gave him the finger. "Nah, I'm just fucking with you, Cuz. You know you're my killa. I told you I got this. Niggaz is looking for you. Fuck you doing here?" he frowned and looked over his shoulder to see if anyone was around to see him talking to him.

"I already know. I had to pay my respects to her, though. She really held a nigga down." Nightmare spoke with sadness in his eyes as he handed him a piece of paper. "That's the address and telephone number to the new hotel I'm staying at." He told him as he looked over the piece of paper.

Taco folded the piece of paper up and slid it into his back pocket. "Alright, Cuz, be careful out here." He gave him a pound.

"Oh, I will. This whole thing is about to be over. I've gotta meeting with The Ghost tomorrow night."

"Word?" he raised his eyebrows.

"Yep, I'm on the move, Loco." Nightmare slid on his shades, turned up his coat's collar, and walked off like he didn't have a care in the world. His collar flapped up against his face from the wind, as he moved across the huge mound that was the cemetery ground.

That night

Darkness claimed the Eastside of South Central Los Angeles. Pimps, whores, hustlers and junkies alike, were all out in full swing chasing their dreams, rather it is in the form of a control substance or small green rectangular shaped papers with In God We Trust printed on them.

Amid the children of the night in secrecy was one Pavielle Hood, slumped down behind the wheel of an olive green '94 Ford Corsica eating Cantonese take-out from Paul's kitchen. He had forked over a gram of crack to a smoker named Smiley for the usage of his car and the whereabouts of a certain someone with some very vital information.

Pavielle had been staking out his mark's crib for the past three hours. At first he thought old Smiley had fucked him on the info part of the deal, but that was until he saw his mark leaving his Lexus truck with two white girls.

Old nigga came through for me, almost thought he'd fucked me, Pavielle grinned as he chomped down the last of his Chow Mein and washed it down with a Coke. He turned on the radio to a Rock n Roll station, as he listened to the music escaping from the speakers; he closed his eyes and mentally prepared himself for the task at hand

***

Taco made his way up the steps of his home with two white girls under each arm. The tanned skinned, bleach blonde, blue eyed bimbos would fit right in with Hugh Hefner's stable of Playboy Bunnies. While Taco was tipsy off shots of Patron and lime, the girls were gone off Cosmetologins and Columbian flake. Back at the club they had tried to get him to do a few lines but he declined. He heard that cocaine produced acne and he was a playboy hustler who prided himself on his appearance.

***

After throwing on his hoodie and Nike Baseball gloves, Pavielle emerged from the Corsica with an AK-47 cradled in his arms. He wasn't worried about being spotted with the husky automatic weapon because most of the street lights were out, or too dim to reveal any souls lurking in the night. Head on a swivel and assault rifle at his side, he moved in on Taco's yard hunched over. He made his way up the driveway with the stealth of a cat.

***

Taco finger popped the short haired blonde while he hit the longer haired blonde doggy style, looking down at his dick dive in and out of her. The longer haired blonde screamed and pulled the sheets as she sprayed the bed with her love juices. Her body then collapsed onto the bed shaking as if she'd been zapped with a taser gun. A smile accented her face having gotten off. A sweaty Taco smacked her on her ass and left a red palm imprint on her left buttock. He then set his sights on the short haired blonde, licking his lips in inticipation of filling that third hole in her face. Carefully, he sat her on the floor and glided his dick down her throat, leaving only his balls hanging against her chin. First, he started with slow, short strokes, and then he worked his way up to long ones. He sped up his thrusts which brought tears to her eyes and caused her to gag.

"Gaaaaaa," Her eyes rolled to the back of her head, making her look like she was being possessed.

"Yeah, bitch, I'm bought to blow your mothafucking brains out!" he told the short haired blonde as he stared into her eyes. "Gangstas," He shouted proudly, throwing up his set as he fucked her mouth even harder, his hips moving rapidly. A river of her hot saliva came running out of her mouth and slid down his hairy nut sack, dripping on the floor. The short haired blonde held the back of his knees and closed her eyes tightly. It was something about being gagged while being mouth fucked that turned her on. She fingered her pussy as he continued to fuck her mouth like it was her pussy, his tongue hanging out of the side of his mouth. Homegirl looked as if she was about to vomit. She gagged louder and harder, feeling that flap of meat between her coochie lips growing stiffer. Feeling himself about to explode, Taco withdrew himself out of the short haired blondee's mouth and blasted her in the face with so much semen that it looked like her face was melting onto the floor. The long haired blonde quickly hopped off the bed and began licking her friend's face.

Man, I love white hoes, Taco thought, loving the idea of the two bitches being so freaky. He smiled as he looked down watching them both handle his dick. One was sucking on his balls while the other was sucking his member. Famished, he wiped the beads of sweat from his forehead with the back of his hand.

***

As Taco rummaged through the refrigerator he heard something upon the roof. He paused for a moment and waited to see if he'd hear it again. Once he didn't, he shrugged and continued his search for some grub, humming the tune of some rap song. He came across a container of leftover shrimp fried rice and a smile stretched across his lips. Unbeknownst to him, while he was searching through the refrigerator, Pavielle had slid down the chimney and into the living room. His face and clothing was smeared with dirt, but he didn't give a fuck. He was there on a mission, so being filthy was the least of his concerns. Pavielle shook off the dust he'd collected on his way down chimney and crept over to an unsuspecting Taco, gripping that Ak-47 with both hands. Taco turned around stuffing his face with rice; his eyes damn near burst from their sockets when he saw Pavielle's threatening eyes. The two men stood staring at each other with tension and fear looming in the air.

Blattt!

A missile shaped bullet ripped through Taco's shoulder and threw him against the refrigerator. He slid down to the floor in agony, holding his bleeding shoulder and leaving a smear behind on the refrigerator. Tears formed in his eyes and threatened to drop, but he bit down on his bottom lip to combat the excruciation.

"Arrrrrr," He squeezed his eyelids shut and threw his head back.

As Pavielle rounded the kitchen counter with his Ak-47, the long haired blondee leapt on his back. He spun around in circles trying to shake her loose, but she was hanging on for dear life. Realizing this, he threw her over his shoulders onto the floor, and that's when he heard a pair of bare feet running up behind him. He spun around and slammed the butt of his weapon into the short haired blondee's mouth, sending a spray of blood and teeth through the air. He then kicked her in the stomach and unleashed a hail of bullets on her petite frame, causing her to dance on her feet before hitting the surface with a thud.

"Ahhhhhh," Pavielle let go of an eardrum piercing scream. He looked down at his foot and the long haired blonde had sunk her teeth into his ankle, breaking the skin. She had a lock on him like a pit bull, so he busted her in the forehead with the butt of his rifle, dazing her. He then pointed it at her torso and opened fire, painting the floor with her little ass.

Pavielle's head snapped up and he looked to the refrigerator, Taco had vanished. He then ran down the corridor toward the back bedroom, his legs looking like blurs while en route. He reached the back bedroom just in time to catch Taco pulling a Mac-10 with an extender attachment from the closet. The young nigga whipped around squeezing the trigger of his weapon, it came to life rattling in his hands. Pavielle dove to the carpet and the bullets chewed up the doorway, spraying the air with splinters. From where he lay on the carpet, the young kingpin hugged the trigger of his assault rifle and let go of a spray of bullets that cut Taco down to the floor. Specks of his blood decorated the walls and the floor surrounding him.

"Fuck!" Pavielle fumed, hoping he didn't just murder his only lead to Nightmare. He picked himself up from the surface and ran over to his victim. He grabbed him by his collar and pulled him up to his brows, looking him dead in his eyes. "You ain't dead, wake up! Wake your punk ass up!" he smacked him back and forth across his face viciously, the sound bouncing off the walls inside of the bedroom. When he didn't respond he smacked him again and again and again. Realizing that he was dead, he let his limp body fall to the carpet. The nigga lay there looking out of eyes that were focused on nothing with a wide open mouth.

Pavielle sat on the bed with his eyes shut massaging the bridge of his nose. He blew hard and brought his hand down his face, licking his lips. Looking up, he spotted a piece of paper underneath an ashtray on the nightstand. He snatched the piece of paper up and looked over it; a smile broadened his face. He stuffed the paper into his pocket and left the bedroom.

Nightmare may as well change his name to zombie because he was a walking dead man.

Meanwhile

Six Mexicans lay on their stomachs with their hands cuffed behind their backs in the living room of their trap house. They all wore worried expressions as they watched Detectives Ortiz and Arsenegger take a survey of the drugs they found when the two unlawfully raided their trap.

All of the eses had extensive rap sheets, so they were looking at some footballs numbers. Time in prison that you'd have to be an immortal to finish; thirty, forty, fifty years to life, the digits flashed inside of the Cholos' heads and they felt like vomiting.

"What do we have there, partner?" Arsenegger asked Ortiz. He was wearing a windbreaker with a bulletproof vest underneath it. A baseball cap with Police on the front of it was turned backwards on his head and he was clutching a shotgun.

"Seven kilos of coke, three bricks of heroin and…" Ortiz picked up two pounds of weed and inhaled them. The aroma brought a smile to his face. "Five pounds of the finest weed you'll ever breathe." He was dressed just like his partner and was toting a shotgun, too.

"You mean four pounds of the finest weed we'll ever breathe," Arsenegger smiled mischievously, stashing one of the pounds inside of his own personal duffle bag.

"Right," Ortiz smiled and gave him a pound, "Four pounds of weed."

"Where are you Vatos from, homes?" Arsenegger asked the Mexican with the shaved head.

The Cholo told him what hood they were from.

"Well, homes," Arsenegger began, addressing a shaved head Mexican. "We don't need to throw in the rest of this shit. The seven kilograms of coke is enough to bury all of your brown asses under the Big House."

"Fuck!" a Mexican with a brow piercing cursed, pounding his forehead against the floor.

"What would you say if I told you, you and your homeboys could walk away from this, scot-free?" Arsenegger inquired, wearing a dead serious expression.

"I'd say, 'What do we have to do?'" shaved head answered.

"I thought you'd never ask." Arsenegger smiled sinisterly. For a brief moment, the Mexicans thought they saw his face turn red and horns grow out of his forehead.

The Vatos had just made a deal with the devil.

Chapter 14

Pavielle watched Nightmare enter through the automatic doors of the hotel from behind the wheel of the Corsica. He pulled his cap down over his brows, turned up his coat's collar, and secured his .9mm inside of his pocket. He was going to get close enough to spit on Nightmare and empty the entire magazine in his face.

Crossing the threshold, Pavielle saw that the hotel lobby was fairly crowded, which was good for him, he could blend right in with the scenery. He followed Nightmare from a safe distance. The last thing he wanted was to get made. He had the element of surprise on his side and he didn't want to fuck that up.

Pavielle peeped from around the corner and watched as Nightmare boarded the elevator. Once the doors had closed he ran over to see what floor the elevator would stop on. The tenth floor flashed.

***

Pavielle ran up ten flights of steps as fast as he could. Once he reached the door with the number #103 on it, he hunched over with his hands on his knees. He was winded and his heart threatened to burst from his chest. He cursed himself for being such an avid smoker. After getting his breathing under control, he cracked the door open and took a peek down the corridor; room #103 was to be Nightmare's final resting place.

Pavielle oozed into the corridor from the staircase door and noticed the hotel maid's pushcart at the end of the hall. He had spent the night at many different hotels and some of the maids kept their key-cards on their pushcarts. Pavielle rummaged through the pushcart until he discovered the key-card for room #103. He then advanced in the direction of his prey's hotel room.

***

Nightmare's hotel room was dark when Pavielle stepped inside. The only visible light was the one illuminating from the cracked bathroom door. He could hear the shower water running inside. Mist slowly escaped from the cracked door and spilled into the living room, rolling over the carpeted floor. Pavielle freed his .9mm from his coat and crept towards the bathroom door. A shit-eating-grin spread across his lips as he thought about the look that would be on Nightmare's face when he saw him. At that moment, the living room light came on startling him, his eyes shot open and his lips peeled apart in shock. He turned around and Nightmare raised up from the couch, firing his Desert Eagles. The gold and chrome hand-guns danced in his hands. Pavielle face twisted in agony as hot lead struck his form, ripping his clothes into shreds. Fighting back the pain, he moved forward returning fire, his banger dislodging empty shell-casing after empty shell-casing. Bullets tore into Nightmare, dropping him to his knees.

From the floor, the gangsta crip raised his Desert Eagle and fired two slugs into Pavielle's belly. He winced in pain, but he was determined to kill his enemy. He weakly lifted his .9mm and squeezed the trigger; the first bullet nicked Nightmare's neck while the second struck his shoulder. Nightmare grimaced and grabbed his neck as he hit the floor. After looking to his bloody hand, he swung his burner around and pulled the trigger, hitting his foe's arm and chest. Pavielle staggered across the floor and collapsed beside him. The two sworn enemies moaned and groaned as they experienced a world of hurt, squeezing their eyes shut and gritting their teeth.

Nightmare scowled at Pavielle, he hated his fucking guts. "Fuck you, Cuz!" he sneered as he harped up phlegm and spat it on him. Pavielle shut his eyes even further as the yellowish goo splattered against his face and dripped from off of his brow.

"Fuck you too, Blood!" Pavielle sneered back and spat on him. Goo dripped from the gangsta crip's brow as well.

Nightmare growled as he grabbed his nemesis by his collar and pressed his Desert Eagle under his chin.

"Goodbye, mothafucka!" he snarled and his nostrils flared.

Click!

The Desert Eagle was empty.

Pavielle grabbed his .9mm and brought it for the gangster crip's head. Nightmare grabbed the .9mm by its barrel and a struggle ensued, tilting the weapon back and forth, grunting. Suddenly, Pavielle pulled the trigger and the gun went off, missing his nemesis's forehead by half an inch. This caused his eyes to shoot open and his heart rate sped up, adrenaline pumping. The hotel's maid walked in and saw the two men tussling and ran down the corridor screaming for help. Nightmare let go of the .9mm, grabbed Pavielle by his collar and head butted his nose, breaking it. A gush of blood flushed from his nostrils. He fell to the floor cupping the lower half of his face, blinded by the sensation of the pain.

Nightmare squirmed on the floor beside him, groaning in agony. His injuries from the gunshots were wreaking havoc on him.

Down in the lobby

A dozen police officers spilled through the doors of the hotel with their guns drawn.

"What floor?" the sergeant yelled out to the desk clerk.

"The 10th floor, room #103!" the clerk yelled back. The officers split up, some taking the elevator and others taking the staircase.

An hour later

The paramedic riding in the back of the ambulance with Nightmare checked his pupils with a small flashlight pen and placed an oxygen mask over his mouth. He then ripped open his shirt and revealed a bulletproof vest. "Son of a bitch!" the paramedic stated, removing the bulletproof vest from Nightmare's person.

"What's that?" the paramedic behind the wheel yelled over his shoulder.

"This guy was wearing a Kevlar." He told him.

"Get the fuck outta here!" the paramedic responded with disbelief.

"Seriously."

Meanwhile

Pavielle lay handcuffed to a gurney in the back of an ambulance, with an oxygen mask over the lower half of his face, barely conscious. The paramedic had discovered that he had a

Kevlar bulletproof vest on as well. He held it up and counted the holes in it. There were a few.

***

The paramedic glanced down at Nightmare and then back to the bulletproof vest. The gangsta crip seemed to have produced a black .32 out of nowhere. Seeing movement in his peripherals, the paramedic looked to him and met his small pistol. He went to scream and a bullet slammed into his forehead, smacking pieces of his skull and brain fragments against the inside of the ambulance. What was inside of his head went running down the wall and outlined the floor. The roar of the small weapon startled the paramedic behind the wheel, causing him to momentarily lose control of the ambulance. He took a quick glance over his shoulder and saw Nightmare blast himself loose from the metal bracelet. There was a cling and sparks flew as a bullet severed the bracelet that held him bound. Within a matter of seconds, he was on his feet and en route to last man in the van breathing besides himself.

"Oh, shit!" the paramedic panicked when Nightmare pressed cold steel to the side of his skull, indenting the skin there. His bladder filled with piss when his eyes shifted up to the rearview mirror and met a pair of evil eyes. "Please don't kill me, man! I've got...I've got..." the terrifying cold steel pressed against his head made the shook man wet his pants. "Oh, God!" he stole a glance at the expanding darkness on his crotch.

"Ram that mothafucka!" Nightmare commanded; spit flying from his big lips.

"What?" he spoke with a shaky voice, hands quivering as they gripped the steering wheel.

"Ram the back of the other ambulance, now!" Nightmare commanded again. The paramedic rammed the other ambulance and sent it tumbling forward, sliding on its side.

The driver of the ambulance Nightmare was in lost control of the emergency vehicle and crashed into a light pole, bending it at its center. The police cars that were trailing the two ambulances to the hospital came to a screeching halt. The police officers hopped out of their vehicles, drawing their guns.

Nightmare shook off his daze and looked to the paramedic; the wreck had knocked him out cold. He kicked opened the back doors of the ambulance open and jumped down into the street. He looked a head and police officers were coming for him. He ran to the driver side of the other ambulance, unlocked it, and pulled the barely conscious driver out from behind the wheel. After letting the driver drop to the street, he climbed inside the ambulance.

The other paramedic was unconscious and bleeding at the head. He moaned and groaned in pain. Nightmare looked to Pavielle and he was still handcuffed to the gurney. He was disoriented and woozy. He removed his oxygen mask and surveyed the inside of the ambulance. He hadn't noticed that Nightmare had climbed in behind him.

Nightmare raised his .32 to Pavielle's head and pulled the trigger.

Click!

The sound of the empty gun grasped Pavielle's attention. Once he looked back and discovered his nemesis, he struggled to free himself from the handcuff. Annoyed, Nightmare discarded his pistol and looked around for something to kill his prey with. His eyes settled on the medical machinery and he ripped the cord from the back of one of them. He wrapped the cord around both of his hands, coiling and uncoiling it, testing it for strangulation. He then smiled wickedly, feeling that it was perfect for the murder that he was about to commit.

As Pavielle struggled to free his wrist from the metal bracelet, Nightmare was looping the cord around his head, pulling it against his throat.

"Yuuuck," Pavielle's eyes bulged and his mouth hung open, veins etching up his temples and neck. He gagged and choked as tears rimmed his eyelids and broke free down his cheeks. He began to turn red in the face as the cord grew tighter around his neck, threatening to cut off his oxygen. He tried to put up a fight but the bullets he took had left him weakened. The ghosts of his mother, father, Panic, Woo, Big Head, as well as a host of other loved ones had began to pop up before his eyes, one after another. He felt something tugging at his spirit trying to vacuum it from his body. He tried to hold on but he found himself losing his grip. A blinding light shined on his face. At first he thought it was a helicopter's light with it being so bright and all, but he couldn't be more wrong.

An elderly black woman in a white gown, with long salt & pepper hair reached out from the light. It was G-momma. She wore a smile on her angelic face. Pavielle didn't know where she had came from beyond the light, but wherever it was she must have been really happy there. She told him that it was time for him to come home. That everyone had been waiting for him. That his mother and father couldn't wait to see their baby boy again.

Pavielle leaned forward, but he couldn't quite reach her; their finger tips brushed across one another. Just as their palms brushed across each other and he was about to grasp her hand, fire crackers went off...

Bap! Bap! Bap! Bap! Bap!

Pavielle looked around disoriented as he gasped for air. Blood was splattered inside of the ambulance. He looked to his feet and there were four police officers with smoking guns on him. He looked over his shoulder and found Nightmare slumped. He was a bloody catastrophe; riddled with bullets. He was the last person Pavielle saw before darkness claimed him.

Chapter 15

"Blood still not answering?" Neck Bone asked from the reclining chair. He, Killa Dre, Ridah Man, and Debo were all at the trap house playing Madden.

"Nah, fuck it," Gouch laid his cellular on the kitchen counter. "He's a big boy; he can take care of himself." He picked up the carton of shrimp fried rice.

"Blood probably somewhere clearing his head," Ridah Man spoke from the couch. He was playing Killa Dre in Madden on the PS4. "He'll come to the surface tomorrow."

"Yeah, Gouch, don't wet it. Booby will be home tomorrow." Killa Dre assured him.

"Blood, fuck all that," Neck Bone interjected, having grown frustrated. "Where the mothafucking weed at?"

Gouch picked up the bag of purple Kush from his lap and tossed it over into Killa Dre's lap, "Roll up, lil' nigga."

"Fuck I look like? All the heads in here," the young nigga frowned, tossing the bag back over to him.

"Nah, you've gotta roll up, Blood," Gouch tossed the bag back. "You're the only Y.G in a room fulla G's so you rolling up; this an O.G call."

Killa Dre sucked his teeth with an attitude and dropped the controller. "Blood, where the swishers at?"

Gouch looked to the empty pack of swishers on the coffee table. "They're all gone, you've gotta roll up to Ace's."

The youngster blew hard and rolled his eyes, annoyed. He didn't feel like rolling to the liquor store, but he didn't have a choice in the matter.

"Don't trip, Blood," Ridah Man told Killa Dre. "One day when you earn your stripes for a G, it'll be your turn to send lil' niggaz to the store," He reached in his pocket and produced a $50 dollar bill, passing it to him. "Here you go. You can keep the change."

Killa Dre stuffed the money into his pocket. He then picked up his car-keys and banger from the coffee table. "I'll be back in a minute." He headed out of the door.

"Yo, who wanna take Killa's game?" Ridah Man asked the living room.

"I'll chip you!" Debo rolled out of the kitchen with a sandwich and Ruffles BBQ chips on the plate resting in his lap. He bit into a chip and picked up the controller.

"You ready for this ass whooping, nigga?" Ridah Man asked him with a smile, feeling like he was about to beat the brakes off of him.

Meanwhile

Detectives Arsenegger and Ortiz sat in their unmarked Crown Victoria at the end of the block from the trap house. They had been staking out the place for four hours now, keeping a watch on things with binoculars from a far.

"One of them is leaving?" Ortiz announced as he looked through the binoculars.

"Who? The head honcho?"

"Nah, it's not Booby Loco. It looks like their young boy, Killa Dre."

An Escalade truck pulled up beside the Crown Victoria, the Mexicans that the dirty detectives had busted were on board. The shaved head Mexican was behind the wheel, he exchanged nods with the two crooked badges before pulling off.

"It's show time." Arsenegger smiled devilishly before following the Escalade truck.

***

The Escalade truck pulled up and parked two houses ahead of the trap house. Shaved head executed the engine. He and his homeboys adopted the masks of super heroes: Superman, Thor, Batman, etc. They then slid on gloves and loaded their weapons with ammo. "Alright, listen up," Shaved head addressed his homeboys. "Me and Joker will take the front. Chewy and Shadow will take the side. Chucky and Spiral you guys take the back, alright?" the eses nodded yes and he cocked the slide on his shotgun.

The eses stormed the front yard of the trap, looking like a crowd of troops storming into the heart of battle. After taking their positions, they adjusted their masks and double checked their weapons.

It was time for some action.

***

"Yeah, nigga, what's up with all that old bullshit you was talking?" Debo talked shit after scoring a touchdown.

Ridah Man scowled, he was pissed off. He hated losing in anything to anyone. "Chill, Professor Xavier, the game ain't over yet!"

Neck Bone was chopping it up on the phone with his main squeeze and Gouch had just lit up another Newport, polluting the air with clouds.

Bloom!

The side of Debo's head exploded into a mass of blood and brain fragments, he slumped over in his wheelchair, dead as a mothafucka.

Boom!

After having a massive hole blown threw it, the front door was kicked open. Shaved head and Joker rushed in like a couple of offensive linemen. Neck Bone scrambled to his feet, pulling his twin .9mms from his waistband, about to get active. Ridah Man dropped the controller and freed his .45 automatic handgun from his 501 Levi's. A shootout ensued between the foursome. Neck Bone took cover behind the La-Z-Boy reclining chair and let his .9mms take turns firing at the home invaders. Ridah Man backed himself in a corner as he let slugs fly from his .45, trying to send them Mexican niggaz off to God.

Gouch dashed into the kitchen to retrieve one of his Berettas from off the top of the refrigerator. He'd forgotten it there when he was rummaging through the refrigerator for his leftover carton of shrimp fried rice. As soon as he crossed the threshold, the window over the sink imploded into glass shards with Chucky coming through it. The back door was tackled open by Spiral; he was cradling a mini Ak-47. Gouch spun on his heels and ran back out of the kitchen, with Spiral spewing rounds from his assault rifle at his ass. Bullets chewed up the kitchen doorway, sending a spray of splinters and debris in the air, narrowly missing their target.

***

"Do you hear that, my friend?" A happy Arsenegger asked Ortiz. "That's the sound of a ghetto orchestra." He referred to the gunshots being pumped inside of the trap house. He pretended to be the orchestrator, moving his hands through the air like he was directing musicians to play their instruments.

"Yeah, these guys better hurry up and get the job done. Maza and Dupri can only hold back the dogs for so long, especially with all of this gunfire. It's enough to wake up the deaf." He said, lighting up a cigarette and blowing out a gust of smoke.

***

Gouch was running out of the kitchen when the side windows in the living room imploded. Broken pieces of glass spilled onto the carpet as Chewy and Shadow came through the windows. They swung the barrels of their weapons in Gouch's direction as he ran for the staircase across the room.

Seeing his homeboy about to be wasted by the two eses, Ridah Man turned his warm gun on the two Chicanos, ignoring Joker and shaved head. He let his cannon rip, leaving Chewy's body looking like something that had been chewed up and spat out. Ridah Man was able to let off one last shot before Joker and shaved head's weapons mutilated his body, making the upper half of him look like it had been hit with a thousand red paint balls.

"Arrghhhhh," Shadow threw his head back hollering in agony. The shot that the dying Blood did manage to get off had struck him right in the crotch. He staggered back holding what was left of dick before dropping off in the corner of the room.

Gouch hauled ass up the steps with Joker and shaved head moving after him, trying to tear his goddamn head off. Neck Bone sprung from behind the La-Z-Boy letting his twin .9mms off on Joker. Slugs ate his bitch ass from the thighs on up. He fell awkwardly and crashed through the coffee table, littering the carpet with broken glass. Seeing his homeboy gunned down, shaved head ran back down the steps trading fire with Neck Bone, keeping him occupied. Neck Bone's lone gunman stance was short lived once Chucky and Spiral joined the firefight alongside their comrade. Once the gunfire had finally ceased and the smoke had cleared, Neck Bone lay on his back gurgling up blood. He stared straight up, blinking his eyes rapidly like he was trying to regain his focus. Right then, a shadow eclipsed him and his pupils shot to their corners. With a scowling face and twisted lips, shaved head stepped to him, pressing his shotgun against his forehead, indenting it. He stared down at him for a time, his upper lip twitching he was so fucking hot. Abruptly, he pulled the trigger and the powerful weapon jerked, blowing his victim's dome apart. Skull and chunks of bloody flesh went flying everywhere, splattering against the ese's pants leg.

Whimpers from the corner of the living room drew his, Chucky, and Spiral's attention. They turned around to find Chewy on the floor holding his crotch firmly, his hands sticky and red.

"Ah, fuck, Chewy!" Spiral shouted after seeing his homeboy's condition, pacing the floor with sorrowful eyes. He kneeled down to his wounded comrade and laid his mini Ak-47 aside.

"I'm…I'm not going to be able to fuck again, am I? Or have kids?" Chewy sobbed, eyes spilling tears and snot dripping from his nostrils. He was whining like a little bitch and looking like a child that had thrown one hell of a tantrum. "My jaina's gonna kill me. I can't live like this carnal." His head snapped around to each of his homeboys, hoping they'd tell him that everything was going to be alright. Snot bubbled out of his nose, he looked scared as shit.

Seeing his homeboy in pain enraged Spiral, he snatched up his mini Ak-47 and stormed up the staircase. He got about halfway up the steps before a shotgun blast sent him tumbling back down in a hurry. His body slammed into the wall so hard that a portrait fell to the floor, cracking down the middle.

"You mothafuckaz came here on your feet, but you're leaving in body bags!" Gouch yelled from the top step, clutching his shotgun as it wafted with smoke. "You mothafucking Wet Backs done broke into the wrong nigga'z house!"

Shaved head and Chucky crept to the steps cautiously. Shaved head tried to take a peek up the staircase and Gouch nearly blew his mothafucking head off. He brushed his hand down his stubble head to feel for blood, eyes wide thinking that he had been hit. He was good though. While Gouch talked shit from the top step, shaved head signaled for Chucky to hand him something. The Vato reached inside his overcoat and produced a throwing grenade, passing it off to his com- rade. Shaved head pulled the pin, waited a moment, and then threw that bitch up stairs.

"Oh, shit!" the eses heard their enemy shout.

Kaboom!

Gouch came tumbling down the stairs a bloody mess, the left side of his face was fried and his eye had discoloration. Chucky spat on his face and kicked him viciously.

"Come on. Let's get the fuck outta here," shaved head nudged Chucky. He heard the police car sirens wailing in the distance. He turned to head for the door and his forehead exploded, bullet flying out the back of his dome. Blood hit the wall behind him and he crumpled to the carpet. Chucky whipped around to start dumping and some hot shit went through his right-eye, exiting out the left side of his skull. He dropped to his knees and fell over shaved head's body. Together their forms created a bloody heap on the floor.

Arsenegger had both his hands wrapped around Ridah Man's hand, which was holding his smoking .45 automatic handgun. "Alright, you can come out now." he called toward the kitchen. Ortiz emerged from the kitchen with two shopping bags: one had bricks of cocaine and the other had $150,000 dollars in it. The plan was to make the murder scene look like a drug deal gone bad.

Ortiz put one bag in Chucky's hand and the other bag in shaved head's hand. He looked to the corner and saw Chewy on the floor, holding his crotch. His eyes were staring out of their corners and his mouth was ajar. He was dead.

"Poor bastard," Ortiz shook his head sadly as he crossed his heart in the sign of the crucifix.

Arsenegger looked over the bodies scattered on the floor. "Where the fuck is he?" his forehead wrinkled with wonderment.

"Who?" Ortiz raised an eyebrow.

"Booby?"

"He's not here." He looked over the faces of the bodies.

"I'm going to check up stairs, you check down here." Arsenegger pulled his gun from its holster and ascended up the steps strategically.

Ortiz checked the living room, the kitchen, and then took a peek through the curtain. There were about four police cars on the lawn. Arsenegger raced down the steps shoving his weapon back into its holster. "Son of a bitch isn't here! Any luck?"

He shook his head no and said, "All clear down here!"

"It's okay. We'll get him, and all the rest of them, too." Arsenegger assured his partner, touching fists with him. He had a dead serious ass expression on his face.

Detectives Maza and Dupri came through the door, guns drawn, flanked by half a dozen police officers. Maza and the rest of the police holstered their firearms once they spotted the necklace badges around Arsenegger and Ortiz's necks. Maza gave Arsenegger a nod and a wink and he returned the gesture.

"Uh, partner," Ortiz called for Arsenegger.

"Yeah," Arsenegger answered, turning around.

"Someone decided to crash another party." He told him, nodding to the space where Gouch's body once was.

Meanwhile

Killa Dre slumped down in his seat as he passed the trap house. There were four police cars and an unmarked car on the front lawn so he figured they must have been raided. As soon as that thought invaded his mind a couple of coroner vans passed him.

Damn, what the fuck happened? Killa Dre thought with a crinkled forehead. Only time would tell what had transpired inside of the trap.

***

All that could be heard in Pavielle's hospital room was the Beeps of the heart monitor. The room was dark save for the light illuminating his face from above his head. He lay in his cast iron-bed in a coma, hooked to tubes and an assortment of devices to monitor his vitals. Death loomed in the atmosphere, the silhouette of the grim reaper moving past the north wall made this evident.

To Be Continued...

Me and My Hittas 3

AVAILABLE NOW BY TRANAY ADAMS

The Devil Wears Timbs 1-7

Bury Me A G 1-5

These Scandalous Streets 1-3

A South Central Love Affair

Me and My Hittas 1-6

The Last Real Nigga Alive 1-3

God Bless the Trappers 1-3

A Gangsta's Empire 1-4

Fangeance

Fear My Gangsta 1-5

A Hood Nigga's Blues

The Realest Killaz 1-3

The Last of the OGs 1-3

The Streets Don't Love Nobody 1-2

The Dopeman's Bodyguard 1-2

King of the Trenches

www.ingramcontent.com/pod-product-compliance
Lightning Source LLC
Chambersburg PA
CBHW070358200726
48294CB00003B/970